H

By: B.M. Hardin

ISBN-13:
978-1981244843

ISBN-10:
1981244840

This book is a work of fiction. Any similarities of people, places, instances, and locals, are coincidental and solely a work of the authors imagination.

Dedication & Thanks

I truly thank the Man above for my gift and for the opportunity to live in my purpose and the courage to chase after my dreams.

I thank my readers for following my work and allowing me to entertain them time and time again. I appreciate their continuous support and their interaction with me daily in my book club: "It's A Book Thing"

I appreciate you ladies more than you know!

This book is dedicated to all of my readers, family and friends, that continuously listen to my book ideas and share their opinions, good or bad. I am who I am, because of ALL OF YOU! THANK YOU!

Her 13th Husband

Chapter One

All I hear is raindrops.

No. Wait. I hear something else.

What's that sound?

Impatiently, I waited for the sound to become clearer.

Suddenly, Jackson started to whisper, as the soothing sound of a saxophone, became easy for me to recognize.

"You can take it off now," Jackson instructed, and hurriedly, I untied the blind-fold.

We were standing in an all-white room with high windows and glass ceilings. There were dozens of long-stemmed red roses, in every direction, and a massive white fur rug underneath my feet. The candles swayed against the cream-colored, velvet wrapped chairs. The saxophonist continued to play as he stood next to the white marble fireplace; home of raging flames that danced to the saxophone's mesmerizing melody.

It was perfect. Everything, was perfect.

I watched Jackson, take a knee, and I knew that tonight, was the night.

His mouth started to move, as he pulled out a small black box, eagerly revealing a diamond ring, but honestly, I hadn't heard a word that he'd said.

I wasn't listening to him at all.

I was listening to the rain.

The rain slammed against the glass ceiling with vengeance. Outside, there was natural chaos, but here, in this space, inside of this place, was peace and harmony.

Jackson tugged at my hand, causing me to remember what was taking place, and I smiled at him. Finally, I allowed myself to receive his words.

"Baby, will you marry me?"

I exhaled and instantly, I nodded my head.

"Yes, I'll marry you," were the words that I said…

Twelve Husbands Later…

"Daughter, it's almost time," my mother beamed at me.

I stood there, laced to perfection, in the strapless, off-white wedding gown, that I'd allowed my friend JuJu to pick out for me. The dress wrapped me with comfort, and I could tell by the look on my mother's face that she approved.

She let out a sigh of delight, as though this was my first time around. As though this was the first time that she'd seen me as a bride.

It wasn't.

"Ivy?" She called me by my *newest* name.

Ivy was my *third* name in the past few years, but it would be the first time that I used it to marry a husband.

I was born Malaysia Christina; and then I became Deena Marie. And now, I was…

"Ivy Raye?"

My mother, or as I liked to call her, Mama Kay, called my name again, and I looked at her.

I gave her half of a smile, and took a deep breath.

Slowly, I approached her, and she handed me the bouquet of roses, and softly kissed my cheek.

"You look beautiful," she complimented me. "I wouldn't have taken JuJu as a woman of good taste," she admitted. "But this dress is perfect!"

I studied her. She looked damn good herself. The gown that she was wearing, hugged her with grace, and I stared at her in admiration. I could only hope that I would look half as good as she did when I was her age. Over the years, she'd aged like fine wine, but finally, she was starting to get a few gray hairs and wrinkles.

"Are you ready?"

"As ready as I was the other twelve times before."

That's right. I was on my thirteenth husband; and saying that I was tired of getting married, was an understatement.

Mama Kay smirked at me, and after she pulled the veil down over my face, she took me by the hand and led me out to where the rest of the wedding party was waiting for me.

The crowd cooed in admiration; well except for JuJu. I heard her yell out, "Oh, hell yeah!" and immediately, she was reprimanded by a few people, for cursing inside of the church.

She was the only person, other than Mama Kay, in the entire wedding party, that was there on my behalf. The rest of the people, and majority of the church, other than a few co-workers, were my soon-to-be husband's, family and friends…because I didn't have any.

My father died when I was young, and after that, it had always been just Mama and I.

The music started to play, and one by one, they all went in. When it was my turn, my feet felt as though they were stuck in cement. Mama Kay pulled at my arm, but I didn't budge. There was something that I had to say to her first.

"Mama?"

"Yes baby?"

"This time, no matter what happens, I want to keep him," I whispered to her, sincerely. "I want to keep my husband."

She patted my hand just as the whole church stood up, and waited for us to proceed. She spoke through the huge smile that was plastered on her face.

"Oh Honey…we'll see."

~***~

"Good Morning, Mrs. Nino Deon Parker," my thirteenth husband grunted. He inched closer to me and kissed my lips gently, once I was within his reach.

"Ohh, Mrs. Parker? I like the sound of that," I assured him, although, my mind instantaneously, began to run down my shameful list of previous last names.

Jones, Smith, Simmons, Floyd, Mills, Lopez, Harper, Feu, Lopez—again, they weren't cousins though, Fleming, Hampton, Gilford.

That was every last-name that I'd ever taken from a husband; other than my new last name, Parker. And it was every last-name that I was trying to forget.

I'd gotten married, for the first time, when I was just nineteen years old to "Perfect Proposal" Jackson.

Jackson Jones was like…well, it doesn't really matter what he was like in the beginning because in the end, he wasn't the man that he'd pretended to be.

At the time, Jackson was over a decade older than I was, but in my mind, all I cared about was the fact that he chose me. He promised to love me and take care of me, at least that's what he'd said.

Losing Daddy from cancer when I was nine, really did a number on me. He'd loved me unconditionally when he was alive, and once he was gone, I started to feel as though something was missing; like a piece of my heart had been taken away from me. And no matter how hard Mama Kay tried to fill that void, she couldn't.

Mama Kay never remarried, nor did she date another man after Daddy was gone, so, no one was there to fill his shoes or to take his place, but secretly, I'd wished that there had been.

I didn't want to say that I viewed Jackson as a father, because that would be disgusting, but from the maturity and love, to the sense of protection, and everything else in between, that's what I saw in him.

That's what he was to me.

I thought that with him, in him, I'd found forever; but I was wrong.

Mama Kay told me that I was too young. She'd told me that I wasn't ready. She'd told me that he wasn't the one for me and she'd told me that I would regret it.

And I did.

I wasn't even used to my last name yet, before he changed. The caring, sweet, loving man that I'd married disappeared, right before my eyes, and every day, a possessive, abusive, cold-hearted man came home to me.

I'd tried to hide it, for a while, though I wasn't sure why, but Mama Kay was like a blood hound and once she picked up on it, she forced it out of me. She told me to tell her the truth. I'd tried to lie, but there was no use. I broke down right in front of her that day. I told her that every day he made me cry, and that sometimes she couldn't see me because I had a black eye. To my surprise, she didn't get upset, at least she didn't show it. She didn't scowl me for not listening to her in the first place. She didn't ridicule me for making a bad decision.

Instead, she asked me two haunting questions.

Two questions that I would never forget.

"Do you still love him?" She'd asked.

I told her that I was no longer sure.

"Do you want him dead?"

She'd asked the question, just like that, straight to the point, and I'll admit, at first, I thought that she was joking. She was as sweet as apple pie, with a heart as pure as gold, so surely, she couldn't have meant it, at least not literally, but she had.

That day, I never answered her second question, but it hadn't mattered. In the end, she made the choice all on her own.

I remembered that day.

She'd come over to our house to visit, just in time to see Jackson in one of his bad moods. He was screaming at me, calling me names, and after refusing to eat his breakfast, because his eggs had gotten cold, he broke every dish in sight, threw a coffee mug at me, slamming it right into my nose and then he'd stormed past her, out of the house, cursing along the way.

Jackson never came back home that day.

That night, I'd gotten a call saying that he'd been in a terrible car accident.

Jackson was dead.

Medical Examiners said that he'd fallen asleep at the wheel. Yet, I knew that he'd gone to bed early the night before, but I didn't ask them many questions.

Instead, I saved them all for her.

Mama Kay smiled once I told her the news, confirming that she was pleased. I already knew that somehow, someway, she'd had something to do with it, and I didn't hesitate to ask her how. She simply told me that it wasn't any of my concern and that knowing less, was for the best.

Then, she'd hugged me, and told me that I was free. She told me that she'd saved me and said that hopefully, next time, love would work out for me.

But that time, for the first time, she'd been wrong.

My husbands got worse and worse and had it not been for Mama Kay "saving me" each time that I married a mistake, I was sure that I would've been dead a long time ago.

Actually, I knew for a fact that I would have.

Mama Kay studied thanatology; death, for years, but she'd retired from being a Forensic Pathologist. Simply put, she knew a little bit of everything, that involved death. She was an expert on the many ways to die and with my marriages, her knowledge had come in handy. That and the fact that she'd told me that she'd cashed in on a few favors that she'd been owed from all of her years of changing lab results and reports for the high and mighty. She'd said that she'd always known that one day, they'd come in handy. To this day, I had no idea who helped her when it came to *taken care of* my husbands, and she told me that I never would. All I knew was that time and time again, I married the wrong man and each time she *fixed* it.

Why didn't I just get a divorce?

Why did they have to die?

They didn't *have* to die; but I would be lying if I said that the world wasn't just a little bit better, without them in it.

Still yet, as the years went by, my husbands continued to die, and pieces of me started to die with them.

"Damn baby, what's on your mind?" Nino somewhat screamed, bringing me back to reality. I smiled at him.

"You," I lied.

Though I'd never actually killed any of my husbands, I'd always allowed it to happen. I'd allowed her to help me get a fresh start, and for that, I'd always felt just as guilty.

But as I stared at Nino, I was sure that I no longer needed her services or her help. And even if I did, I made a vow to myself, as he twisted the ring on my finger, that no matter who or what he turned out to be, I would never ask.

Finally, I had to live with my decisions. I had to live with the choices that I made like a normal person should.

And that was all I'd ever wanted…just to be normal.

14

A normal life, with a normal husband, being a normal wife, with normal problems, that were solved with normal solutions.

That's what I wanted the most.

And even if we ended in a divorce, that would be okay too; as long as no one else died because of me.

Nino started to kiss me, and I shook away my thoughts and turned my attention back to him.

Out of all of the husbands that I'd ever had, Nino was the one that I enjoyed the most, sexually. I'd had a lot to compare to, but the freaky things that he had bottled up inside of him, intrigued me and I loved that he always wanted to try something new. I was addicted to him and I looked forward to having him please me, in his own weird, exciting way.

"I love you."

"I love you too," he said. I felt his manhood start to swell up against my thigh, and I assisted him with taking off my panties. Once he was in position, he kissed me, aggressively, and he waited for me to beg him to put it in.

Once he was inside of me, Nino took his left hand, and placed it around my neck. Lightly, he started to squeeze.

"Baby? The tighter I squeeze, I want you to scream," he whispered in between kisses. "I want you to scream:

Help me! Help me! As loud as you can and beg me to stop."

I looked at him confused.

What in the *special victim's unit* type of shit is this?

For a moment, internally, I screamed at the thought of the possibility that I'd married a psychopath; but then I started to remember all of the other *not so* normal things that we'd done in the bedroom, and I realized that this one request, just didn't compare. We'd done all kinds of crazy, unspeakable things to each other with our tongues, our fingers, hell, a butter knife and even a wire hanger. So, this request, technically, wasn't all that bad.

The truth to the matter was that it reminded me of someone else, and of an incident in my past, that I'd spent a few years trying to forget.

The death of husband number nine.

After the death of my first husband, I married what seemed like every year, or every other year. I guess my husbands' just hadn't expected "until death do us part," to come so soon. After the death of my 6th husband, I changed my name, for the first time, to Deena Marie, and Mama Kay and I moved to a new state and city.

But a change in location, still didn't change my luck with marriage and men, and after three years, and two more dead spouses, I bumped into husband number nine.

Honestly, I thought that I was done. I really thought that he was the one.

I was a few months from turning 30. I'd long since finished my degree and at the time, I'd just landed my first 6-figure salary position.

I felt accomplished. I felt hope.

And I'd vowed to Mama that I was done having her clean up my mess, and whatever came next, good or bad, I would simply have to deal with it.

Humph. There I was trying to be normal again.

Yet, there was nothing normal about my 9th husband.

He was the son of a millionaire and…my boss's son.

His name was Dave.

They owned a huge Social Media Management firm and accurately put, he was a walking checkbook.

He was Caucasian, and because I was Black, I wasn't so sure that my boss approved of our relationship, but against my boss's wishes, and maybe even warnings, I started to date his son.

Dave appeared to be a perfect fit for me.

Outside of him being one of the most handsome guys that I'd ever met, we'd had a lot in common. We shared so many similar qualities, and we made each other laugh. We'd both had our share of marriages, though I only told him about two of mine, and conveniently, I'd left out the fact that both of the husbands were dead.

Dave had been divorced, twice, and at that point in his life, he seemed to know what was required of him to be a good husband. So, after dating for a short while, we went for it.

That time, I'd had the wedding of my dreams.

It was massive; something fit for a queen. And that's exactly how he made me feel, before and after we were married. He made me feel special. He did everything I asked of him. Gave me things that I'd never even thought to ask for. He truly made me feel like royalty…but it was all a show.

Only a few months into our marriage, I discovered the truth about Dave. I found out that he was only flaunting me as his queen, because secretly…he preferred another *king*.

Dave was gay, bisexual, open-minded, or whatever the hell he wanted to call it, and the truth to the matter was that he wasn't as in to me being his wife as he was as in to me being his cover up.

When I came across the homemade porno of him and the man that I'd known to be his best-friend, I was devastated.

I confronted him. He didn't deny it. Instead, he asked me to accept it. He asked me to roll with it and to let him feed his desires, every now and then, and in exchange, he would continue to be the husband of my dreams, and he promised that I would never want for anything.

Needless to say, I couldn't accept it and I told him that I was leaving him. Having him killed hadn't even crossed my mind. I was just going to pack my things, divorce him, and start all over again.

Dave could have cared less that I wanted to leave, as long as I kept my mouth shut. As long as I kept his little secret. Dave's father, my ex-boss, was a very stern, faith-based, religious man. Dave knew that he would never accept his only son being with a man. He knew that he would disown him, and see him as a disgrace.

So, Dave requested to buy my silence…and I got angry. We got into an argument and I told him that I would expose him to his father and that's when everything took a turn for the worst.

Dave attacked me.

He started to choke me.

He went on and on about his father, and that he'd worked too hard for his approval and that he could never find out the truth about him. Disowning him, being shamed by him, being cut out of his will, just wasn't an option for him. Dave said that he wouldn't allow me to ruin his reputation or his life.

I tried to take back my words and my threats, but he wouldn't listen. He told me that he just couldn't risk me telling anyone his secret and for that reason alone, he couldn't let me live.

I'll be honest, I thought that it was my karma.

For all of the things that I'd stood by and let happen. For all of the dead husbands, whose blood was somewhat on my hands. For all of the deaths that I'd given the okay to do. I thought surely, him choking me to death was my punishment.

I remembered trying to peel his fingers from my neck as he squeezed. It didn't take long for me to realize that he wasn't going to let up, and I was just going to give up. I was going to accept my fate and just let it be.

I was going to die.

But suddenly, I got one last wind, and though our maid was only God knows where inside of our 7500-sq. foot home, with all of my might, one last time, I cried out for help…

And thankfully, my cry was heard.

There was a loud thud and then he fell to the floor beside of me. And there stood Mama Kay.

Breathing hard, I glanced at her and then at him.

He wasn't dead; at least not yet anyway.

"Mama---,"

"You called for help," she'd said. "Come on. We have a plane to catch."

I looked at her confused.

"He's fine. Just a little bump. It didn't kill him. Now, get up and come on."

Wanting to get as far away from Dave as possible, being that he'd just tried to kill me, that day I grabbed my purse and I left him, lying there on the floor, already knowing in the back of my mind that I would never see him alive again.

Mama Kay wouldn't tell me how she knew what was going on at that very moment, but she did assure me that everything was going to be okay.

Within an hour, we were on a plane to Florida, where we then boarded a ship for a cruise. Mama Kay was obsessed with them, cruises, and she'd told me for a month that she was going, and though I'd declined, she'd said that she always purchased two tickets, just in case I changed my mind.

I was out of reach for a whole week.

I never tried to call Dave and he never tried to call me; mainly, because he was dead.

He was found with a suicide note and a bottle of pills beside of him. The note revealed his inability to be who he really wanted to be and that he couldn't live in his truth, without suffering the consequences. He didn't write too much, never actually confessed his transgressions or his secret, but he'd said enough. He'd said that he was giving up. The note said that he was miserable, and with his therapist confirming, what little she could, of his issues with depression, and fear of not being accepted for who he was and who he really wanted to be, no questions were asked, and his death was ruled a suicide.

And though the cops didn't have any questions for me, I did ask Mama Kay a few. Surely, Dave had some help with the whole suicide thing, so I asked her what she'd done, and her response had been: "Nothing…really."

She told me that she'd sent him a little encouragement to get him to do it himself. Whatever the hell that meant.

I wasn't sure how, but whatever had been done or said to him, it worked. And I guess in a way, his death worked out for me too, because combined with his properties, assets, and insurance policies, he made me a very, and I do mean very, wealthy woman.

Total, Dave left me 15.3 million dollars, and though it had been years since his death, I still had plenty of it left.

The lack of air circulating to my lungs, brought me back to the matter at hand. I struggled to breath as Nino started to pound and as he continued to squeeze.

"Say it baby. Say it."

I wasn't sure if I could.

He squeezed harder, tighter, and I grabbed him by the hand.

"Help me! Help me!"

"Louder!" Nino growled.

"Help me!" I screamed as loud as I could. My cries of fake, but somewhat real distress, seemed to fuel Nino's penis, and he drilled it inside of me like a jackhammer. Unfortunately, I couldn't focus on the pleasure, because I was too busy focusing on trying to breathe.

I closed my eyes, and waited for it all to be over.

"Uggggh!" finally, Nino grunted, loudly, as he released himself inside of me. Sweat from his forehead dripped onto my face, and he wiped it off, just as he collapsed onto the bed. He was satisfied, and smiling from ear to ear. "Damn, baby. That was good, wasn't it?"

I nodded, knowing that I hadn't enjoyed it at all.

Nino kissed my forehead and then he got up.

I watched him, lustfully, as he headed towards the bathroom.

He was average height, only a few inches taller than I was, but his body was fascinating. You know how pleased you are when scrambled eggs turned out just right; all yellow, light and fluffy and stuff?

That's how satisfied I was with Nino's appearance and physique. His chest was big and full of tattoos, and he had delicate, covetous abs, with just enough muscles to match. Nino was light-skinned, with a kissed by the sun, glow, along with honey brown eyes, and big, succulent pink lips. The shape of his eyes and bushy eyebrows, along with his full, tamed beard, caused him to look a tad bit mysterious; as though he was always thinking about something or keeping a secret. And I loved the high, wild, fade that he often wore with his hair.

"Baby, are you sure that you don't want to go on a honeymoon?" Nino screamed from the bathroom.

Personally, I'd gone on one honeymoon, too many. And quite frankly, I wasn't in the mood to pretend as though it was my first time going wherever it was that he would've wanted to go.

When Dave died and once his millions were in my bank account, I'd figured that I deserved a break from my sad, destructive reality. So, for a whole month and a half, Mama Kay and I, went everywhere, anywhere, that our hearts desired. We made tons of lifetime memories and new experiences, together. Just the two of us, just the way that it had always been.

And even with all of the traveling, I still had plenty of money left; not to mention that Dave wasn't the only husband that I'd collected money off of after his death. And because I pretended not to have it, I rarely got the chance to spend it.

Nino had no idea about the amount of money that I had stashed away.

When Mama Kay and I moved again, here to Virginia, I went right back to work. I worked a corporate job and lived paycheck to paycheck just like everyone else. I liked things better that way. I'd tried revealing my money to husbands ten and eleven, and both of them confirmed for me, that it was just better to let people believe that you were living, struggling, and maintaining, just like they were.

So, that's what I did.

"No. We don't need a honeymoon. I'd rather stay here for the next two weeks and try to get pregnant," I screamed back at him and I heard him chuckle.

"Okay, baby. Whatever you want. Whatever you say."

I was sure that if Nino wasn't it, then no one was.

And my mind was made up.

If this marriage failed, I was going to adopt a baby, buy a vibrator, and a lifetime supply of batteries and just live out the rest of my days, with my money, my Mama, and husband-free.

Some would probably want to know what had taken me so long to get to this space or why I hadn't stopped trying my hand with love a long time ago. They might even ask why I kept getting married, especially after all that had been done and knowing that every man that married me, ended up dead.

Why didn't I just give up?

And my question to them would be: Would you?

After all, who doesn't want love?

Who doesn't want a happily-ever after?

What woman doesn't want to marry the man of her dreams and spend the rest of her life with him?

It wasn't my fault that my dreams somehow always ended up turning into nightmares, but I'd had to try.

So, that's what I did.

I kept trying, but after getting married thirteen times, finally, I was done. I wasn't buying another wedding dress. I wasn't taking another last name. This was it for me. And if it wasn't, I was ready to accept the fact that some things, just aren't meant to be.

Unfortunately.

~***~

"So...how is everything going?" Mama Kay grinned, as she ate the cucumber from her fork.

I stared at her. She seemed to be acting a little strange. Something about her was different.

"Everything is fine. Nino is perfect."

"No one is perfect but God, Sweetie," she said, and snapped at the waitress. "But I'm glad to hear that."

I waited for the waitress to refill her cup and once she walked away, I replied to her.

"I want you to know that I was serious about what I said on my wedding day. No more dead husbands. No more mysterious deaths or accidents. This is it. He is it."

"You said that the last time. And a few times before that."

"I know, but this time, I mean it. I'm not getting married anymore, Mama. And I don't want anything to happen to him. Okay?"

She chuckled. "I'm not the only one who needs to hear your little speech. Let's not forget that you asked me to have your last two husbands "taken care of"", she said making parentheses movements with her fingers.

She was right, I had.

Instead of her suggesting, stepping in, or somehow causing the deaths to happen without my permission, I'd asked her to do whatever it was that she did, to my last two husbands, but I'd had my reasons.

"You're right. I did ask, the last two times. And now I'm asking you, no matter what happens, no matter what we go through to leave this one alone. I don't want to talk about doing anything, if things go bad. I don't want you to feel the need to save me. Whatever happens, I just want you to let it be."

"What if he turns out to be like husband number four? Ohh, or like number seven?"

"Mama!"

"Okay. Okay. Okay. Fine. You have my word. I won't interfere this time. In fact, whatever issues you guys go through, do us both a favor, and keep them to yourself. He's all yours." She took another bite of her salad. "Besides, I won't be around much anymore, anyway. I'm moving away."

I looked at her.

Mama Kay and I, had lived in 5 different states, over the last twenty plus years. We moved for the first time after Daddy died; Mama took a transfer position within her job. And then we started to move to different states after every few dead husbands of mine.

What little family we did have left was all the way on the West Coast and that was on my father's side; Mama Kay had cut her family off years before I'd even come into the picture.

So, all we'd ever had, outside of Daddy for a couple of years, and outside of my husbands, was each other.

"Moving? Where?"

Mama Kay looked at me. "Ivy, I have a confession. I've been married for the last two years, chile. And I'm ready to just let you spread your little wings and fly, so that I can go settle down and spread these old legs of mine. Mama has needs too, you know."

Mama Kay blushed as my mouth dropped open.

"I just needed to make sure that you were okay first. You've always been my top priority. Always will be, and I needed to make sure that you were safe and happy."

I continued to stare at her in confusion.

Married?

I'd never, ever, seen her go on a date, or even talk to a man in a romantic type of way after Daddy. And now, all of a sudden, she was saying that she was married? For two whole years? And she didn't tell me?

"Married?"

"Um huh. I think you were still dating husband #10 when we started to hook up. I can't remember. We would travel back and forth, just to…you know. Those cruises and little trips that I would take by myself…I wasn't always alone. Sometimes, he would be with me. And then two years ago, we got married. It started as a conversation, and then a suggestion, and then suddenly, this ole' Mama of yours was hitched!" She squealed, and then kept talking. "I always wanted to stay close to you, just in case you needed me…which you did. And I didn't want to tell you since you don't seem to be all that lucky in the husband department. I didn't want you to get discourage."

"Two years Mama?"

"We eloped. Neither of us wanted to do the whole wedding thing anyway. He's been patient with me, but patience runs out, daughter," Mama Kay chuckled. "It's time to focus on me, just a little bit. So, I'll be moving to Louisiana."

"What? Louisiana? When?"

"The end of this week."

"Mama!"

"You'll be fine, Ivy. I'll be a phone call and a plane ride away. Besides, I think you finally found him. I think Nino will be for you, what your father was to me. I think he's the one. And you know, that I've never thought that about any of your other husbands."

Well, that was the truth.

She'd disliked something about all twelve of my deceased husbands, so to hear her say that about Nino, meant a lot to me.

"Chile, your taste in men is *God-Awful*! But, I like Nino. And though I've tried, I can't seem to see find a thing wrong with him. He's the one, Ivy. It took a while for you to find him, but finally, I believe that you have. Besides, it's normal to have to kiss a few frogs, or kill a few husbands, before you find your prince; as long as you find him. That's all that matters. And even if you didn't, whatever you decide to do about him, is totally up to you."

I looked at her for a while, just to try to process things.

"And I'll be riding out the storm, with my husband, no matter what, right along with you. No more dead husbands; for either of us."

It took me a minute, but, finally, I exhaled and then I smiled at her.

"I don't know what to say. I'm surprised, to say the least," I said to her, and she shrugged. "Maybe I should say congratulations."

"Thank you, daughter," she said.

We were both quiet for a few moments.

"I guess now, the only question left to ask is when do I get to meet, my *not-so* new stepdaddy?"

I giggled as Mama Kay took a sip of her drink.

"You've already met him."

I looked at her confused.

"He's your dead husband's father…husband #6," she gulped her drink.

What the hell…

"Mama!"

She shrugged and then started to grin.

****

Chapter Two

"Good Morning, Ivy. Excuse me, it's *Mrs. Ivy*, now, right?" Cage, my next-door neighbor, bellowed.

I ignored his sarcasm, and I stopped walking, for just a second, just to admire him.

Cage was the most beautiful man that I'd ever seen!

He was like Christmas Morning; all dipped in warm, hot chocolate. His skin was melt in your mouth smooth and he was as dark as the minute before midnight. He had a head full of curly hair that reminded me of dyed wool, and eyes that were sexy and daring, and revealed the secrets of his soul. His smile was so hypnotic, and whenever he flashed it, for a few moments, I felt powerless and somewhat in a daze.

Everything about him was perfect.

For over a year, we'd had this weird sort of thing going on. We flirted with each other, talked all the time, touched a little, here and there, and even one night, we shared the sweetest, most intimate, kiss that I'd ever endured.

I'd wanted him so badly that I could taste him, but for whatever reason, no matter how much we talked, laughed, and teased each other, he never tried to take it to the next level. The attraction was there. The connection and the intimacy between the two of us was undeniable. Still, Cage, never made a move. I believed that my vagina craved him even more than I did, and even when I would clearly throw myself at him, he would always be…what's the word…

Respectful?

It confused the hell out of me!

And then I met Nino.

One morning, Cage spotted him coming out of my house. He gave me a strange look, as though he was jealous, but then when I saw him, later on that day, he laughed. He admitted that he'd just gotten up the nerve to ask me out on a date and that he was disappointed that he was too late.

I'd tried to explain to him Nino and I, were just friends at the time. All he'd had to do was say the word. Honey, I would've dropped Nino's ass quick, fast, and in a hurry. But yet again, Cage shied away, and that date invitation that he'd spoken of, never came.

And even after all of that, and even while glancing at the 2-carat diamond ring on my finger, I still wanted to *sample* him. I swear, I still wanted me a piece of that damn man!

"What's that shining on that finger over there," Cage smiled. He'd known that I was getting married. I'd told him one day, a few days before the wedding. I blushed, and hid my hand behind my back.

I didn't want to talk about me, or Nino or being married. I just wanted to enjoy lusting over him, without feeling guilty about it.

"Should've been you," I flirted with him.

Cage flashed his spellbinding smile.

"Maybe it should've. He's a lucky man," he said and then he turned to walk away.

I watched him in desire and disappointment, until he disappeared.

"Depends on what you call lucky," I mumbled, and then I headed back into the house.

It was moving day for Nino.

Since the house that I was renting, was bigger than his, he'd decided to move in with me, until we found a house to purchase.

I'd moved into the house, right after changing my name to Ivy, and right after burying my 12th husband.

Paul.

Paul was an older man. And I loved the fact that he already had kids. I'd always wanted a house full of kids, so being with him, gave me a chance to experience something like motherhood, even if it was just for a little while.

Paul was successful, cool, calm and collected, but he hadn't been completely honest with me about why his first marriage hadn't worked out. He'd forgotten to tell me about his little drug problem. And what a horrible problem it was!

He'd hid it so well too. I never saw it coming. I never would've guessed it, and I didn't. In due time, he just got tired of hiding it.

Paul started coming home high.

He owned two very successful businesses, and he had plenty of money to maintain his habit, but I just hadn't signed up for everything else that had come along with it.

There were times that I might not see him for days, and then he would scroll into our house, like everything was okay, demanding sex from me, when only God knows what could've been floating around inside of him. And then after hours of arguing, he would fall into a hibernating sleep and piss in the bed, all over me.

So, we fought. A lot. About his habit, about the lack of sex, on both ends. We fought about everything.

I was going to leave him. That was my plan.

I wasn't going to tell Mama Kay anything. I was just going to leave. Paul would get to live. He would get to be a father to his kids; partially high most of the time, but still, he would be around. But he caused more problems than there had to be.

Knowing that I was unhappy, and in hopes of securing his finances, after I told him that I wanted a divorce, he started checking up on me. He started asking questions, and he'd even paid someone to try to dig up a little bit of dirt on me, only to find out about my dead millionaire husband, Dave.

He accused me of baiting and trapping him. He thought that it was a money thing; even after I explained to him that the millionaire husband that he'd found out about had left me plenty.

I told him that I didn't need his money or want anything from him. I told him that we were over, but he continued to be a pain in my ass. I got tired of arguing with him, and since he wouldn't leave, because it was his house, one day, I started to pack my bags.

I suppose he was high on whatever it was that he liked to use, but the more and more that I packed, the angrier he became. He started unpacking my things and throwing them in the trash.

Finally, I gave up, grabbed my purse and tried to head for the bedroom door, but he grabbed me. I tried to fight him off, but he held me tightly, and then he tried to kiss me.

I refused him, and after tussling with me for a while, he lifted me off of my feet and threw me onto the bed. I continued to fight him, and all he did was laugh. And I mean, he laughed loud, and hard as though he found what he was doing to me to be funny. And then abruptly, the laughter stopped. He started to rub his hands all over me and no matter how much I cursed and tried to push him off of me, he didn't budge. Instead, Paul held me down, and forced himself inside of me.

He raped me.

Husband or not, I said no, I screamed no, and he took what he wanted anyway.

Once he was done with me, distraught and in a rage, I ran out of the house. That time, he didn't try to stop me. I arrived at Mama Kay's that night, crying. I was angry, more than I'd ever been before and with pain in my heart and still in between my legs, I asked her to make the pain go away.

And however, she does, what she does…she did.

She'd told me to go to sleep that night, and the next morning, Paul was found dead from an overdose, with the needle still in his arm. And that was one death, that I didn't feel bad about. I didn't feel sad at all.

Being that he'd been found at our home, I concluded, that somehow, Mama Kay had someone staging the deaths; to look like one thing, yet she'd probably caused the deaths by something else, because Paul never, and I mean never, did drugs at home.

I couldn't be sure how she always got it done. All I knew was that none of my husband's deaths ever looked bad on me. I was never a suspect. Either the deaths looked as though they'd done something to themselves, or it was a death by accident, or a wrong place at the wrong time scenario. And I was never anywhere near them at the times of their death, either by design or by coincidence.

So, therefore, there were never any questions for me.

None of their family members ever blamed me.

No one ever had anything other than sympathy for me.

There was never anything suspicious on my end; partly because I truly wasn't doing anything.

Mama Kay was.

Nevertheless, Paul was dead, and thankfully, he hadn't given me anything. And once he was in the ground, instead of moving out of the state this time, Mama Kay followed me to a few cities over, and that's when I changed my name, again, and became Ivy Raye.

And ever since then, I'd been here, at this house, with a new name, new job, and now, with a new husband.

I stared at the reflection of myself in the full-length mirror, just as Nino's truck pulled into the driveway.

My complexion was a tinted cocoa brown, and the melanin seeped through every crevice of my skin. My face was round, with a timid set of brown eyes, and a small button nose, accompanied by a lazy smile that was attractive, but somehow, it always appeared to be forced. I had a mole on my left cheek, and a scar on the right one, that had been given to me from husband number seven. I wasn't the perfect size, nor did I have the perfect shape, but I had just enough meat, where it mattered the most, and curves that had come along with age, that I was starting to adore. I was far from a model, but I cleaned up well; maybe even a little too well, since men always seemed to flock in my direction.

Obviously, getting a man, or finding a husband, for me, was easy; it was keeping him alive that was the problem.

I turned my attention back to Nino.

He was smiling, genuinely smiling, as though he was filled with so much joy. He oozed with happiness and all I wanted, at that moment, was to do something to make him even happier.

I hurried by the front door, once he started to head up the porch steps. I got down on my knees, just as he turned the door knob.

He giggled once he saw me.

"Ivy? What are you doing?"

Immediately, I started to tug at his belt.

"Drop the box."

"What?"

"I said: drop...the...box."

Once his belt was undone, and he saw me working on the button and zipper, he dropped the box, just as he was told.

"Baby," he mumbled, but immediately cooed once I placed him inside of my mouth. For a while, he tried to move me away from the front door, but I wouldn't budge.

I continued to suck, slurp, and spit on his *mic*, until finally, he relaxed and allowed me to take him to a place of pure ecstasy.

I secretly smiled, at the sound of his moans.

Now, this is how you celebrate moving in together. I mean, getting carried over the threshold of the door was cute and all; but christening the moment with good, doorway *sloppy-toppy*, was even better.

~***~

I looked back at Nino.

He was fast asleep.

The neighbor's, on the right side of us, had a dog that was barking continuously. I listened, and waited, for it to stop and when it didn't, I got out of the bed.

I peered out of my bedroom window, which faced nothing but the small, thin row of trees that separated my yard from theirs.

I could see the dog, but I couldn't see what it was barking at, until…

"Whoo!"

I jumped as a dark shadow, hurried across my window. The figure pushed past the row of trees in a hurry, as I rushed out of the bedroom, and headed for the living room, to see where it was going. By the time I reached the window, the figure was running up the street. There was a car waiting for them. I couldn't tell what make or model the car was, but I was sure that it was blue…or maybe it was black.

The car sped off, and still, I stood there for a while, wondering who they were, why they had been there, and what the hell they'd been doing, snooping around at 4 a.m.

Finally, and after checking the locks on the doors, I headed back to bed, and after snuggling close to Nino, easily, I drifted back off to sleep.

~***~

"How long did you take off from work?" JuJu asked.

JuJu was the only woman that I'd allowed into my personal space, and that I'd let get close enough to me, to call her a friend. I hadn't really had any friends since I was a teenage girl.

Throughout the years, especially in the work place, I'd mostly stayed to myself. Mama Kay had always been my best friend. I was satisfied with knowing that with her, I didn't have to pretend, but when JuJu and I crossed paths, I just couldn't help myself. The energy that she gave off was undeniable, and even the meanest, coldest, snobbiest, person in the world wouldn't be able to ignore her.

You just couldn't help but love her.

And I loved me some JuJu!

No matter how much I tried to ignore her at first, I couldn't. She was loud, and crazy, and everything that I wanted to be. She was smart as a whip, funny, and on top of all of that, she was as sweet as a bowl full of honey, and a damn good listener too.

"I took two weeks off. We're not going on a honeymoon though. We're focusing on getting pregnant," I confessed to her.

"I know that's right! Why are you even on the phone with me? You should be somewhere with your ass up in the air."

I chuckled.

"You and I both know that you only have a few good years left. Hell, you better hope that it's not too late already," she laughed. "If it is, I've got a few eggs that you can buy. It doesn't look like I'll be using them anytime soon."

"Shut up, JuJu." I was only in my mid-thirties. There was still time, at least I hoped there was.

"Nino, with his fine ass, better get busy! Tell him he has a job to do, and future God Mommy JuJu, is counting on him to get it done. And I hope the baby come out cute, because you know all babies ain't cute, I'm just saying."

I was appalled that she would even let something like that come out of her mouth, considering that she was…ugly.

And I do mean scare the hell out of a baby or small child type of ugly. JuJu was so ugly that you couldn't look at her too fast early in the morning, or if you looked at her for a long period of time, your mouth would start to water, and you had to redirect your focus, to keep from gagging.

Don't get me wrong. She had a to-die-for personality, beautiful hair and an astonishing smile, but when God was passing out beauty and good looks…she must've been in the bathroom. She sure as hell missed that blessing. She just wasn't attractive at all! I guess he made it up to her though by giving her a few extra portions of booty; mine included. JuJu had enough ass to feed a small country. She just wasn't easy on the eyes.

But I loved her ugly ass though.

"So, you know I hooked up with one of the groomsmen in your wedding," she revealed.

"Shut up! Who?"

I was shocked!

Who in the hell had been desperate enough to lay down with somebody who looked like that?

"His name was Clarke, I think."

"Oh yeah. He works with Nino. I've met him a few times. He just went through a divorce," I said to her, hoping that she got the hint that he was probably lonely, horny, and desperate, so she shouldn't expect him to come calling her for seconds.

"Are you going to see him again?"

"I doubt it. We didn't exchange numbers. In fact--- aww hell, here comes Jarret. He probably wants me to do something that his lazy ass should be doing. Let me call you back."

And with that JuJu was gone.

I grinned as I placed the phone down.

Jarret, our boss, the only person in the office that was above me, had been wanting to fire her ass for as long as I could remember. She was only there because of me, and though he was technically in charge, I knew that he got the feeling that if he let her go, then I would surely leave too.

Heading into the kitchen, I paused once I noticed Cage in his backyard. He was cutting the grass. I tiptoed towards the window, and hid behind the curtain, so that he couldn't see me gawking at him.

The sun lit him up like a roasted Christmas Tree, and as he pushed the lawnmower back and forward, the movement of his big, strong back, and his edible arms, unexpectedly, started to turn me on.

I tapped my foot, once I felt my clitoris develop its own heartbeat. I tried to stop looking at him, but I couldn't help it. I noticed that I was drooling and I closed my mouth. He pulled his hair into a ponytail and took off his shirt.

Damn it! That did it!

If I couldn't have him physically, my vagina convinced me to settle for him mentally.

My hand found its way underneath my dress. I wasn't wearing any panties, and the warmth of *her* welcomed my fingers with open arms. The juices from my arousal, embraced my fingers, and before I'd even realized it, I'd lifted my leg, and placed it on the edge of the kitchen sink.

I refused to take my eyes off of him, as my fingers found my spot. Obediently, they went to work and I moaned as my mind started to play tricks on me.

It played images of things that at that moment, I wanted to see. Images of Cage. Images of Cage doing everything that I wanted him to do to me.

Unable to visualize, the way that I wanted to, I forced myself to stop watching him and I closed my eyes.

Yes. I could see it.

Us. Together. Hot, and sweaty, rolling around on the freshly cut grass. The thoughts were so vivid, that I could almost smell the scent of grass on his skin. I cooed as I imagined the way that he would feel inside of me and like a crackling fire on a cold Winter's night, my body temperature heated up and I knew that the inevitable was coming, way too fast and way too soon.

I breathed faster, harder, as my fingers went into overdrive and then finally, as though there had been a mighty flood, I released my sweetest nectar from the deepest part of me. My aftermath cuddled with the spaces in between my fingers, and as my breathing steadied, finally, I was able to open my eyes.

I looked in the direction of Cage…who was looking directly at me.

My mouth opened wide, but somehow, I forced myself to close it. Embarrassed, I wondered how long he'd been standing there, watching me, and if he could tell what I'd been doing.

I didn't know what to do, so I just stood there, leg still up, frozen in place, wishing that I could disappear.

Luckily, he didn't linger. Cage grinned at me, wiped his face with his shirt, and then he pushed the lawnmower into his garage and went inside.

Hurriedly, I took my leg down, and pulled down my dress. As I started to wash my hands, I chuckled at myself. "Until next time," I said in my mind.

~***~

"Why are you so quiet?"

Nino rubbed the side of my face.

"Are you missing your Mama already? She'll be fine, Ivy. She doesn't have a husband. Her daughter just got married. Maybe she just feels like it's time for her to start living her own life. You know?"

I heard him, but I didn't reply.

And he was wrong.

She *did* have a husband; who just happened to be my ex father-in-law. But of course, I said none of this to Nino and I didn't have any plans on mentioning her marital status to him, unless I had to.

I still couldn't believe that she'd married him, Simeon, my 6th husband's father, knowing that she was behind his son's death. I'd asked her how she could look at him, talk to him, and marry him, knowing the truth. And all she'd said was: "It's not like I was the one that pulled the trigger."

Whatever helps her sleep at night, I guess.

She'd said that on one of her solo cruises, she'd ran into him on the ship. She said that he recognized her, and that they started to chat, and from there, they hooked up, a lot, and then he asked her to be his wife.

I was still surprised that she'd said yes.

Once Daddy died, in my opinion, Mama Kay was never quite the same. I believed that the fact that she knew so much about death, yet she couldn't save him, caused something to change inside of her. Or maybe it caused something that was buried deep inside of her to revive.

When my father was first diagnosed, she'd gone through this period of crazy research, hoping to find something that might save him. And even after he died, she continued to let it all consume her for quite some time; death, poisons, cures, you name it, it had her attention.

Until my issues became her project.

Simeon was younger than Mama Kay, which made it all the more surprising that they were an item.

I knew for a fact that he was younger than her because he'd always talked about how he and my deceased husband's mother had gotten pregnant in high school; so, he'd only been 16 years older than his son.

Mama Kay was so seasoned, and so mature. I was surprised that she didn't intimidate him.

Hell, she intimidated me!

But I loved her. And I was happy that she was finding a life outside of me. And for the most part, though it was different, I was happy that she was gone.

"I'm fine baby. I just miss her. I'm used to seeing her all the time, you know?"

"Yeah baby, I know. Well, she can come and visit anytime. You wanna know something funny? I almost thought I saw her today."

I looked up at him.

"Yeah. I know it's crazy. But I thought I saw her, right before a truck ran a red-light and almost hit me head on. I thought I saw her siting in her car not too far away from me."

"A truck almost hit you today?"

"Yeah. Almost. I swerved just in time. Nobody was hurt and by the time that I looked back in that direction, the car and the woman were both gone," Nino shrugged. "Of course, it wasn't her, but that lady sure did look a hell of a lot like her though," Nino became quiet, as I thought about what he'd said.

Was Mama Kay still in town?

She'd left for Louisiana days ago. I'd been the one to drop her off at the airport and everything, but what he'd said about the truck stuck out to me.

Most of my husbands, more than half of them had died the "accidental" way. Car accidents, falls, and one even died from "drowning"; at least that's what the reports said.

So, the truck running the red light was right up Mama Kay's alley of "Oops...he's dead!" types of deaths.

She wasn't trying to kill Nino behind my back, was she?

It wouldn't be the first time she'd killed a husband of mine without telling me why or what was going on first.

My 3rd and 4th husbands, for example, died without her telling me what she was up to first. I hadn't known that she'd given them death dates, until after it was over. Once they were dead, she revealed to me that husband #3 was having an affair on me with his secretary, and three other employees. So, one night, after work, she set up a mugging and had him stabbed as he left. And husband #4, may or may not have had a thing for little boys, according to Mama Kay, so she had him killed just in case.

She hadn't told me before hand, but in her words, she was just doing what was best for me, and saving me as always. She'd said that she would always be protecting me, even when I didn't know it.

But we'd talked about Nino, and nothing was supposed to happen to him.

She wanted me to be happy, and I was. I really was. She'd promised to keep out of my marriage and to stay away from my husband.

She'd promised that she wouldn't try to hurt him.

She wouldn't lie to me…would she?

"Make love to me."

"What?"

"You heard me. Make love to me," I demanded Nino, hoping to silence my thoughts.

I opened my legs and welcomed him inside of them.

Nino grinned as though he'd found his own little piece of Heaven, as he crawled on top of me.

"Give me a baby," I whispered to him. All at once, I was attacked by emotions, and I wasn't quite sure why. "Please. Just give me a baby."

A single tear escaped from my left eye, and he caught it with the softness of his lips. He didn't say a word, but it was as though his heart was conversing with my soul, assuring me of the love that he had for me. And for the next fifteen minutes, he showed me.

Nino made love to me like he never had before. He made love to me as though he was trying with everything that he had in him, to give me what I wanted. To give me my heart's desire. And in that moment, at that very moment, I loved him more than I'd ever loved anything and anyone, in my entire existence.

I loved him more than me. I loved him more than I loved her.

After we freshened up, Nino told me that he was taking me to dinner, but just as we were about to head out, he got a phone call and asked if we could postpone it.

"It sounds really important. You know that he's been going through a lot, with the divorce and all. Order take-out, and keep it warm for me. I'll be back before you know it," Nino said, as he kissed me and headed out the door.

Once his car was out of sight, I found my phone and called Mama Kay.

"Hello Daughter," she greeted me.

"You aren't trying to kill Nino, are you?"

"No." She answered quickly, and then started to giggle at something Simeon said. I then heard him tell her to tell me that he said hello, but she ignored him.

"Is everything okay?" she asked.

"I guess so. Call me when you're done." Even in concern, I couldn't help but to smile.

Mama Kay was in her sixties, but she didn't look a day older than forty, forty-five at the most.

She was the definition of beauty, charisma and poise; even with her deadly little secrets. She had the face of the angel, the skin of honey and butter, but she was a tall as an oak tree. Her long, stringing hair, swayed when she walked as though they were branches with black and spotted gray leaves. The amount of knowledge that her brain possessed was unheard of and just by looking at her, you could tell that she was as clever as a fox. She didn't have one single health problem at her age, not one, and I was convinced that she would be the one to bury me, instead of the other way around. I was positive that she would outlive me and now, she would have someone to do it with.

I never imagined that she would remarry again.

Though she'd married Daddy, Mama Kay has always had problems with men. And it all started with her father.

From what she told me, he, my grandfather, was an evil man. Thankfully, I never got the chance to meet him. He was dead long before I was even thought of and he was dead because of her.

Mama Kay told me that he did horrible things to her and her mother. He was the man of the house, the king, and they had to treat him as such. They had to obey him. They had to serve him. And both of them had to *please* him. He did whatever he wanted to do to her, and her mother hadn't done a thing about. Mama Kay said that her mother was scared of him, they both were, but Mama Kay said that one day, for her, it all changed.

It changed when her mother had a late child; Mama Kay's younger sister. Mama Kay said that she was almost sixteen when her mother got pregnant and had a new baby. She called her sister my Auntie Fay. But Mama said that by the time her sister turned two, she noticed their father starting to take interest in her. She noticed him looking at her, his own daughter, with the same lust in his eyes that he'd had for her and she knew that it wouldn't be long before he started doing to my Auntie Fay, what he'd been doing to Mama Kay for years.

She knew then that she was going to have to stop him.

That's when her journey of finding out as much as she could about death began.

Mama Kay studied it. She breathed it. She needed it, because she knew that his death, was the only way to change their lives. She was getting to the age of where she would be able to leave home, but she just couldn't leave her mother and sister behind...not with him.

Not with him alive.

Mama said that she became obsessed with findings on poisonings, how to make deaths look like accidents, and everything else in between. She'd said that she thought about how she wanted to do it for weeks, and then it was as though it was fate for her to kill him, because she said one night, out of nowhere, the perfect scenario presented itself to her.

Every third Saturday, her father worked around the yard. Her mother, my grandmother, had been complaining about the roof of the barn, for weeks, saying that it was raining in on the chickens and the hens, so Mama Kay said that she woke up early, and greased the bottom of his work boots.

That morning, she offered to complete her outside chores, first, once she saw her father grab his ladder. She explained the barn as being quite big and tall, so she knew that he would be climbing high up to reach the roof; high enough for a fatal fall.

Mama Kay told me that she watched him, in disgust that day, as he placed on his tool belt, and started up the ladder. She told me that she'd started to hum the same tune that he hummed, while he molested her, as she headed in his direction.

During her research, she'd found that ladder falls were pretty common accidents, and most of the time, the victims…died.

It was perfect.

No one would ever question a thing.

She'd hoped that he would fall all on his own, before she reached him, which is why she'd greased the bottom of his shoes, but unfortunately, he didn't.

She'd described herself as feeling liberated as the wind blew through her hair as she sashayed towards him. She'd said that she didn't feel an ounce of guilt because in her mind, she was doing what was right and what was best. She was saving them. She was delivering them from evil, were her exact words.

And I knew that in her heart, she'd believed them.

She really thought that she was doing the best thing for all of them, and that she was saving her sister from a world of trouble, hurt and pain. She was saving her sister from turning out like her. She never denied being emotionally damaged from all of the rape, physical and verbal abuse. She knew that she had problems within herself that would take a lifetime to heal, but she refused to let it happen to someone else. Not if she could stop it.

Mama told me that her last living memory of her father was of him looking down at her. She remembered the wrinkles in his forehead and the dark puddles, that he had for eyes, staring down at her, as he stood at the top of that ladder. She said he didn't say a word, but once she smiled at him, she'd said that his face was painted in confusion.

And then she said with all of her might, she kicked the ladder from up under him, stepped back and watched him fall.

She admitted to hearing a few bones break and the snap of his neck as she'd turned her back to him. She told me that the wind had blown just one last time, as though the universe was on her side.

She walked away from him that day, knowing that her mother wouldn't bother him, or even come looking for him for hours, until supper was hot and ready. And by then, he would be and was a long time…dead.

But Mama Kay confessed that his death wasn't as satisfying as she'd hoped it would be. It didn't take away the memories or the pain. And two days after his funeral, which was her 18th birthday, she just went away.

She said she hitchhiked a ride, with a bag and the clothes on her back, and never looked back. She never saw her mother or sister again, but at least she knew that they were safe. At least she knew that they were free.

Mama Kay never told a soul about what she'd done that day, except for me; which she told me the story, the day after my first husband's death.

I believed, that in her mind, she truly believed that she was saving me from my abusive, no-good husbands, and in a way, over time, I started to believe that she was too.

Coming back to reality, I exhaled and placed my phone on the counter, but just as I started to walk away from it, it started to ring.

It was JuJu.

"Hey---."

"Ivy! Come quick!"

JuJu was breathing hard, and I asked her tons of questions that she ignored. Finally, she spoke again,

"Ivy...Nino is..."

~***~

"And you didn't see anything? Anyone?"

Nino shook his head. "It happened so quick. I was heading to my car, the car came out of nowhere, and ran me over. I don't know much else."

Nino talked to the police and I sat in silence beside of him. He'd been involved in a hit and run, and he'd been hurt pretty badly. It had been days, but he had a broken arm and shoulder, bruised ribs, sprained ankle, a concussion and his left eye was swollen shut, so the police had delayed their questions.

I had a few questions of my own.

What was he doing there with JuJu?

When she'd called me, she told me where they were, and I arrived at an outside café.

When I got there, Nino was on the ground, unconscious, being checked on by the medics and JuJu was only a few feet from him, flustered and concerned. I hadn't had time to ask questions then, since they were preparing to load him onto the ambulance and I had to leave with him, but I had plenty of time and questions now.

He'd lied to me.

He'd told me that he was going to meet one of his friends, but he was there with JuJu?

Why?

I seemed to be more concerned with that little fact, other than the fact that he'd been ran over and almost died.

"No one else saw anything either. Nothing except the car. A green car, dark tinted windows. They didn't even have a license plate on the vehicle after reviewing the camera footage. But we're working on it. That's it for now. We will be in touch as soon as we find something."

The officers left the room, and I closed the door behind them.

"Can you believe all of this? They just ran me over like some stray dog, and drove away. I can't believe that I'm not dead." Nino said disturbed.

"Why were you with JuJu?"

"What?"

"You lied to me. Why were you there with JuJu?"

I stared at him, but he didn't appear to be nervous.

"I wasn't there *with* JuJu. She just happened to be there too. I went to meet Clarke, just like I said, but he never showed up. I got a beer, and a table, and I waited. JuJu saw me sitting there, and walked up to me. We exchanged maybe two complete sentences with each other. I got up. Told her that I was headed home to you, and headed for my car. And that's when…"

I looked at him with suspicion.

He looked at me with reassurance.

He waited to see what I was going to say or ask next, but I didn't say anything. I could tell that more than likely, he was telling the truth.

"And no offense, but have you seen JuJu? I know that's your friend, and all, but I'm just saying, she's a little…" he didn't have to finish his sentence. We both started to laugh.

I exhaled and shook my head for thinking the worst in the first place. Finally, I was able to feel for him what I should've been feeling from the very beginning.

"So, now that we got that out of the way, you scared the crap out of me."

"I know baby, I know. I was scared too."

"And there's no one, that would want to run you over, on purpose, right?"

"No. Not that I can think of."

"That's just crazy. Tinted windows, no license plate, it just doesn't seem…"

"Random," Nino finished my sentence. "To go through all of that, it seemed planned. Set up. But why?"

That's a good question.

I looked at Nino and all of the bumps, bruises, and everything that was broken.

On the day that it'd happened, I'd called Mama Kay, angry and crying hysterically, and still, she assured me that she wasn't involved. She swore that she hadn't put anyone up to hurting Nino, and even offered to get on a plane to come and see about him, but I talked her out of it.

After a few more questions, I was convinced that she wasn't lying to me. I was convinced that she wasn't trying to kill my husband.

So now, as Nino closed his eyes to go back to sleep, I was stuck, pondering the answer to one single question.

If Mama Kay wasn't trying to kill Nino, then…

Who is?

****

Chapter Three

"Clarke, you don't have to stop talking when I come into the room," I said to him, as I reached both of them a plate of breakfast. Nino chuckled.

"Nah, it's nothing like that, Ivy. I'm sure you don't want to hear about my problems," he said.

I'd thought that Nino would've felt some type of way towards him, after he didn't show up at the café, the day of the hit and run. Maybe had he been there, it never would have happened. I was sure that in a way, Nino would blame him, but he hadn't.

"Take care of him while I'm gone, okay?"

"Will do."

Clarke had come over to sit with Nino for a while, since I was finally going to go into work. After kissing Nino goodbye, I was on my way.

I called to check in on Mama Kay as I drove, but she was busy with her husband and told me that she would call me later. It was definitely something to get used to. Since she was unavailable to talk, I turned up the radio, and tried to prepare myself for what I already knew was going to be a long day.

"Glad to have you back," JuJu proclaimed once I sat at my desk.

After the hit and run, I'd taken an additional two weeks off of work, and after four weeks, of not punching a clock, a part of me didn't want to come back.

"I can only imagine how many e-mails I have to go through. How have things been with you?"

I'd talked to her a few times since the incident, and her story was the exact same as Nino's. She'd been going to pick up her take-out order, spotted him, approached him, and as he left, that's when it all happened.

There were still no leads on who had been driving the car, or why they'd run him over in the first place. And I had a feeling that things were going to stay that way.

"I'm doing just fine. I guess. But you get settled, I'll be back later," JuJu said, and she strutted away.

I stared at her, until she walked into her office and closed the door behind her. She'd said that she was fine, but the tone in her voice had said something different. The loudness, the enthusiasm, the excitement for life...was missing. Something was off about her, something just wasn't there.

I'd noticed, but I didn't follow behind her to ask questions. When she was ready to talk about it, I would just be ready to listen.

I turned on my computer, and once I got it up and running, I huffed as I stared at my inbox full of messages.

1,627 e-mails!

"Great. Just freaking great!"

I took a sip of my coffee, got up to make me another cup, knowing that I was going to need it, and then I dived into the e-mails, starting from the top, and working my way down the list.

I worked in a top position for a digital marketing firm and I couldn't say that I enjoyed it, but I did enjoy the atmosphere.

Suddenly, after about an hour or so in, a suspicious e-mail address, caught my attention.

The sender's e-mail address was: thetruth@aboutivyraye.com

What?

Why was my name, Ivy Raye, a part of the domain?

Before I clicked on the e-mail, I headed to do a web search, using only the ending of the e-mail: aboutivyraye.com.

An all-black screen with the words "HA HA!"

plastered across it, popped up. It was the only thing there.

What the hell is this?

I headed back to the e-mail.

The subject line caused me to feel uneasy.

"I KNOW THE TRUTH."

I opened the e-mail, but the body of the e-mail was

blank, empty.

Hmm.

I did a quick search, only to find that I'd received and

e-mail from the mysterious sender, at least once a day, for

the last two weeks, and after a little more digging, I found

that the e-mails started on the same exact day of Nino's hit

and run accident.

I opened the e-mails one by one.

Of every e-mail, the bodies of them were empty; but

the subject lines consisted of:

I'm watching you.

I know who you really are.

Do you need help?

Don't try that.

You are so beautiful.

Is he dead?

Wait. Is he dead?

Were they referring to Nino?

I gasped and scooted away from my desk.

Who in the hell sent these to me?

Why were they watching me?

And they said that they knew the truth…just whose truth were they referring to?

My mind was racing, and my thoughts were all over the place.

Whoever this was, had put in some time and effort to get my attention. And from the looks of it, I was getting plenty of theirs too. They were obviously watching me.

Were they responsible for what happened to Nino?

Where was this coming from, and why now?

I couldn't seem to think straight, as I started to think of all kinds of possibilities.

Was I safe?

Did this have something to do with me? Nino? My dead husbands?

I picked up my cell phone.

Nino was barely 50% back to himself, so I contemplated on if it was a good idea to tell him. He hadn't stopped talking about the incident since it happened, he was barely eating, or sleeping, unless he took medicine, and maybe worrying him, with this, wasn't the best move.

Maybe it wasn't the best time, especially since I wasn't exactly sure as to what *this* actually was.

I could tell Mama Kay.

But then she would come running. And yet again, she would become consumed with my life all over again.

After thinking for a little while longer, I decided not to call her either.

I concluded that I was just going to print out the e-mails, and take them to the police, but not before I sent a reply.

I couldn't seem to stop typing, as I asked question after question, and then finally I hit send.

I waited all day for a response, but it never came.

And at the end of the work day, I printed out the e-mails, and checked one last time.

Still…nothing.

~***~

"What's going on with you?"

"Nothing."

I spoke to JuJu.

"Don't lie to me. I can tell."

She exhaled. "It's nothing. Really."

"Come on. Spill it."

"It's just I feel like…I feel like everyone has something, or someone, but me."

I looked at the phone, and then placed it back on me ear. JuJu never really showed emotion. She was always the life of the party, but Mama Kay once said that those were the people that were hurting the most.

"JuJu, your time for love will come."

"But when? I watch everybody else in love. Getting married. Hell, some people get married, divorced, and just like that, they get married again."

Hell, was she describing me?

Of course, she didn't know the truth about my past, but that was the story of my life. I'd date for a few months, maybe a year. They would ask me to marry them. We would get married, and months later, after they started showing their true colors, they would be dead.

And then it would all start over again.

Though, I didn't have the problem of finding love, well, of love finding me, I understood where she was coming from.

"It's like some women can find, two and three husbands, and I can't seem to find one! No one wants to love me; like genuinely love me. Some days, I just sit and wonder when? When will it be my turn? When?"

Her words were breaking my heart.

I'd been married to some terrible men, but I didn't know how it felt to feel unwanted. I knew how it felt to be abused and mistreated, but I wasn't familiar with how it felt to feel like no one wanted me.

"JuJu, you are amazing. And someday, someone, will see that and girl when they do, they're going to make you the happiest woman in the world!"

"Do you really believe that?"

"I know that."

I heard her start to cry. I got the feeling that she wasn't telling me everything, or at least not saying everything that she needed to say.

"Maybe if I was more like you…"

"What? What does that mean?"

JuJu didn't answer me.

"What does that mean JuJu?"

"I just meant that men flock to you. They gawk at you. They stare at you. You can't deny how pretty you are. And if I was more like you, or looked more like you, maybe they would stare at me too. Maybe then, I could have any man that I wanted."

"You can have any man that you want now, JuJu."

"No, I can't."

"And why is that JuJu?"

"Because one day, he saw you…"

~***~

"Nino, are you asleep?"

His snores answered for him.

I exhaled loudly and rolled onto my back.

A few more weeks had rolled by, and though he was pretty much healed, we hadn't had sex yet…not even once!

If I came on to him, either he pretended not to notice, or gave some kind excuse before I could make a move.

Maybe he was still in pain, or maybe he just had a lot on his mind, and maybe sex wasn't one of them.

I could understand that.

But my vagina couldn't.

And it wasn't like I didn't have a lot on my mind too.

I was concerned about Nino and what had happened to him. I was still receiving the mysterious e-mails, and the police had yet to figure out where they were coming from. And on top of everything else, I was disappointed that a long while ago, I'd gotten a negative pregnancy test.

I'd been praying that all of the newly-wed sex had done its job, but it hadn't. Now, I was ready to try again.

Maybe I would've been fine if he would have at least touched me, but he wouldn't even do that.

He just didn't seem to really be all there.

"Nino?" I shook him. He groaned and then started to snore again.

"Fine. I'll do it myself."

Of course, his snores were his only reply, so I rolled my eyes, and prepared to get down to business.

Nino had always been so sexual, so I only pleased myself when I was bored, or when I saw Cage...

Oh, yes, Cage.

He was my orgasm inspiration.

I thought about what he'd been wearing earlier that day, when I saw him.

He'd still been in his work uniform. He worked in construction. The vision of him, still in his uniform, with a few buttons undone, and still wearing his hard hat, was all that I needed, to get me going. And once I got started, I didn't stop until...

"Ohhh! Yes! Cage! Yes!"

Realizing that I'd said my words aloud and not inside of my head, my eyes popped open, and hurriedly, I looked in Nino's direction.

I waited, and waited, and once Nino let out a small snore, finally, I was able to breathe.

Oh, thank goodness!

Imagine trying to explain that!

Nino and Cage had spoken a few times, but Nino wasn't all that friendly. He was a sweet guy, to those that knew him, but he wasn't the type of person to go out of his way to make a new friend, especially since he'd known all of his for years.

Satisfied and relieved, I turned my back to Nino, with a smile on my face. And before I knew it, I'd fallen into a deep sleep, only to have the morning sun awake me a few hours later.

Still in the mood, I turned to face Nino.

He wasn't snoring, so I knew that he was awake, and if he wasn't, I figured that I could wake him up in my own special way.

I got on my knees, and turned him over. He smiled, and wiped his eyes as though he'd still been resting. I reached for his most prized possession, and he swatted at my hand.

"What?"

He didn't answer me, so I freed his *wood* from his briefs, and positioned myself right above it. I stroked it as I looked at him. I waited on him to moan, but he didn't.

"Nino?"

He looked down at me. I looked down at his limped penis in my hand. "What's wrong?"

Nino didn't respond.

"It's not getting on hard. I used to could look at you, and you would be ready to jump my bones. Now, you can't even get a hard on for your wife? What is it? What's wrong? Is it me? Do I not turn you on anymore?"

I sat up, and released him.

He sat up beside of me.

"No. It's not you. It's me," he started to explain. "It's just…I don't know. I haven't been feeling like myself. The incident, the hit and run, got me bugging."

"That was weeks ago, Nino. And you are fine."

"Yes. I'm fine, but I got lucky. I could've died. I should've died."

"But you didn't."

"You can't tell me how or what to feel about it Ivy. It happened to me. Not you."

"So? But are you going to dwell on it forever? Or are you going to get over it and move on?"

Immediately, I regretted what I'd said. Once I heard the words aloud, they did sound pretty insensitive.

Nino huffed and stood up. "Wow. Good talk. Thanks for understanding wife," and with that, he walked, slash hopped, into the bathroom, and slammed the door behind him.

"Ugghh!" I flopped backwards onto the bed.

Our first argument as husband and wife. And I knew that it wouldn't be our last…especially if he didn't come off of the goods anytime soon!

If I'd been hit and ran over, and didn't know why, or by who, I probably wouldn't want to have sex with him either. I would probably feel the exact same way that he did.

I guess I was being a bitch.

I took a deep breath and headed towards the bathroom door. "Come on, let me in," I knocked, and then turned the knob. I heard the lock click, and I pushed it open.

"I'm sorry. I was being a bitch, insensitive and selfish," I apologized to him.

His face instantly softened. "I'm sorry too. I promise, I'm going to make it up to you. I don't know what's wrong with me. I mean, it was the hit and run, and then…"

"And then what?"

"Some strange shit been happening lately. It has me all bent out of shape. I guess I've been letting them get to me more than I thought."

"Things? What things?"

"Nah, don't worry about it. It's all good. Nothing for you to worry about."

"Don't tell me not to worry about it. What things?"

"For one, I'm pretty sure somebody is watching me. When I go out to take out the trash, or go to the car for something, it feels like a set of eyes are on me all the time. The other day, I went for a drive, for the first time, since everything went down. You were at work, I wanted some stuff from the grocery store, and with my leg feeling a little better, I drove myself. I was in there for all of five minutes. I came back outside and my truck door was open and the chairs had been soaked in gasoline."

"Gasoline?"

"Yeah. A lot of it too. And it was a match on the driver's seat. It looked as though it had been lit, but for whatever reason, it hadn't caught fire. Maybe they threw it in, thinking it was going to burn up everything, but the match went out. I looked around, but I didn't see anybody."

I waited for him to continue.

"I called Clarke, to come get me."

"So, your car isn't really parked at Clarke's like you said?"

"It was. Then he dropped it off for me to get it detailed. They said it was going to take a whole week to get it right. Somebody tried to set it on fire. This shit crazy man," Nino groaned.

Nino walked past me, back into our bedroom.

"And the other day, I'm pretty sure that somebody was inside of the house."

"What?" I asked him.

"I took a pain pill, and laid down on the couch. I dozed off. I don't know how long I was out. But you know that space between the kitchen and the hallway, that always creaks when you step on it? Somehow, I heard it. The medicine had me so far gone, and at first, I could barely open my eyes, but after getting them to open just a little bit, I saw someone, clear as day, walk down the hallway."

Nino stepped into his gym shorts.

"I jumped up. I got myself together, and once I was able to get off the couch, I limped through the house, checking every room, but no one was in here. I starting to think that I was crazy. Maybe I had been seeing things. But by the time I made my way back into the kitchen, I found the back door unlocked and still cracked open. Somebody was in the house, Ivy."

I looked at him in fright.

I knew that now, was the perfect time to tell him about the strange e-mails on my work computer, but I couldn't seem to open my mouth.

What the hell is going on around here?

"I got something for them if they come back though." Nino reached at the top of the closet and opened a box. I knew that he had a gun, but I'd never seen it. "We might need to get you one too."

He closed the box. "And on top of everything else, I got a call yesterday, saying that I was being let go. I lost my job. Some bull about them downsizing."

"Oh no Nino, why didn't you tell me?"

"It just doesn't make sense. I've been at that place for over ten years. I'm the best goddamn CPA that they had. And they let me go? Ivy, things just ain't sitting right with me."

And I seconded that.

"Don't take this the wrong way, but things didn't start going wrong until after we got married," Nino pointed out.

"Yeah. I was just thinking the same thing."

Though the bulk of the craziness was happening to Nino, because of the e-mails, I got the feeling that it all had something to do with me. I wasn't sure why, or how, or who, but I knew that it was somehow, in some way, all my fault.

"You don't have some crazy lover hanging around or and ex that wants me out of the way, do you?" Nino asked.

Hurriedly, I shook my head.

No husband, sorry, but all of my exes are dead.

~***~

"$300,000 is a hell of a wedding present," Nino screeched and I pretended to agree.

"So, this whole time, your Mama was sitting on all of this cash?"

I'd lied to Nino and told him that Mama Kay had given us the money as a wedding present, to purchase a new home. Of course, it was my own money, but it was easier to lie to him and say that it was from her, than to tell him the truth about me.

I just wanted to get out of this house, as fast as possible, and it made no sense to me to continue to live there, possibly in danger, when I had more than enough money for us to move.

"Well, she cashed in on a million-dollar life insurance policy, when my father died, and let's just say, she never really had anything to do with it. She worked while I was growing up, and made good money too, so, it just sat in the bank. And she said that she would rather us spend it on a house, to be safe, versus living here in fear."

Nino nodded his head. "But for the record, I ain't scared. I'm waiting on someone to come back in here," he made sure that part was clear.

"I know baby. And…I was thinking that you could use, $50,000 of it to open your own CPA firm." I genuinely smiled at him, and awaited his reaction.

"What?"

"You heard me. We will find a house, but $50,000 is yours to get your own company up and running. Maybe you can take all of your clients away from the assholes that fired you. And regardless of what you say, you're taking the money and doing this for you, and for us, Nino. And I'm not taking no for an answer."

Nino looked at me with adornment.

"I…I don't know what to say."

"Just tell me you love me and smack my butt."

"I love you," he said, kissed my lips, and smacked my booty just like I'd told him to. I giggled, kissed him again and then pulled away, but he pulled me closer to him. He continued to assault me with his tongue and the budge in his pants told me that his dick had risen from the dead.

Yes! Thank Goodness!

We continued to kiss each other, roughly, and just as we started to tug on each other's clothes…

"Knock! Knock!"

No!!!

Both of us whined, at the sound of JuJu screaming from the other side of the door.

"Let's just let her knock. She'll go away," Nino whispered.

JuJu knocked again.

"Now, we both know that she won't," I laughed at him. "And remember, I called her to come over to fill me in on what I missed in today's meeting at work. I have to be ready for my client tomorrow."

Nino pouted and nodded his head.

I fixed my clothes and eyed him until he started to do the same.

"I hope that we can finish this later."

Nino kissed me. "Oh, yeah. Believe me, you're going to get this *wiggle-jiggle*," Nino laughed and I squealed in excitement as I headed for the door.

"Helloooo!" JuJu screamed and knocked harder.

After our last conversation, JuJu seemed to be back to normal. She explained her comment, saying that some guy that she'd been interested in, a friend, met her one day for lunch, yet he saw me walking in and he asked her who I was, and asked me if I had a man.

Naturally, I guess it'd made her feel some type of way, but I was guessing that now she was over it because she'd been on level 1,000 for the past few days, and because I loved her personality, I was enjoying it.

"Y'all in there being nasty, ain't you? It's hot! Open up this damn door!"

"Okay! Okay! Okay! Stop knocking! I'm coming!" I yelled, as I turned the knob of the front door.

I opened the door, just in time to see her smile, but then...

BANG! BANG! BANG!

JuJu's smile froze. Time stood still for a few seconds, too long. No one moved. No one made a sound. No one breathed. No one said a word.

Finally, my eyes found JuJu's and instantly, my heart started to break.

Her face was confused.

Saddened. Weakened. And unsure.

The blood started to paint her cream blouse a crimson bloody red, and then slowly, she started to fall. She fell forward, right into my arms, the weight of her body, slowly taking me down to the ground with her.

Suddenly, a sound that was so unfamiliar to me, escaped from my lips, as I shrieked so loud that my throat started to burn.

"Nooo! JuJu!"

This wasn't real. This just couldn't be.

This was a dream. It just had to be.

I closed my eyes, and prayed that I was right, but the feeling of Nino rushing past me, running outside, confirmed that I was wide awake.

The gunshots had been real.

The blood all over JuJu was real.

The visual of her taking her very last breath was real. And the pain from my heart breaking was too.

~***~

"Oh, Mama," I ran to her, and threw myself into her arms.

We'd just arrived at the church where JuJu's funeral was about to be held. I'd told Mama Kay that she hadn't had to come, but of course, when we walked in, she was right there waiting for me. She allowed me to sob for a while, and then she pulled me away from her to look at my face.

"Everything is going to be okay."

I didn't believe her. She was telling a lie.

JuJu was dead, and I didn't blame anyone but myself.

Though we had no idea as to who was responsible for the shooting, she was only there because of me. Because I'd asked her to come. Because I'd called out of work to concentrate on lying to Nino about the money.

It was all my fault that she was gone.

I glanced at Nino, who was standing there, waiting for me to tell him what I needed him to do.

After crying for a few seconds longer, I spoke to him.

"I don't think I can do this. Get me out of here, Nino. Please, just get me out of here."

Nino, Mama Kay, and I left JuJu's funeral, before it even got started, and headed for the hotel. We'd been staying there for the past week; since our home had become a crime scene.

"Someone is trying to kill you, or me---or both of us," I mumbled as Nino drove. "They were at our house. They were waiting. They weren't trying to kill her. They couldn't have been. They were waiting for one of us. They'd been waiting for that door to open to take their shot. JuJu had just been in the way."

I was still weeping.

She was my one and only friend.

I just didn't understand.

"They had to have seen me. They were trying to shoot me, not her," I continued to whine.

"No." Nino said. "No one is trying to hurt you, Ivy. I'll never let that happen. Besides, all of the crazy shit has been happening to me, remember? If they were hoping to shoot anyone, other than her, it would've been me."

"No." I shook my head. "Something crazy happened to me too."

"What?" Mama Kay, who had been dead silent, spoke up.

"I've been receiving some weird e-mails at work. They started a while back. They started on the same day that you got hit by the car."

I looked at Nino, who was looking back and forth between me and the road.

"They don't really say much, except that they are watching me, or that I'm beautiful and once, they even asked me if you were dead." I left out the part about them saying that they knew the truth, and the custom domain name that included my name. I didn't know what all of that was about and since I still had secrets to hide, it seemed better if I just didn't mention it, at least not to Nino.

"And you didn't think that I needed to know this?"

"You were already going through so much. Already on edge. So, I printed out the e-mails and took them to the police. I tried to get a reply out of them. I e-mailed them back, so many times that I lost count, but they never respond to anything that I say. They simply wait a few days, and then send something else, completely random."

"Get me the e-mail address. I may know someone that can trace it," Mama Kay said.

"The police tried that already. It's a dead end. Whoever is sending them, knows exactly what they're doing and knows how to cover their tracks."

The car grew oddly quiet.

"Is there something that you aren't telling me, Ivy? Anything? Anything else? Is there anything else that I need to know?"

I could feel Mama Kay staring a hole in the back of my head.

"No. That's it. Well, other than one night, after we'd just gotten married, someone was snooping around the house, but I couldn't be sure if they were in our yard, or the neighbor's. So, I didn't bother to mention that either. I didn't see them. Not their face. Just the back of them as they ran away."

Nino growled and fussed for a while.

"Is that it Ivy? Is that all that I need to know?"

"Yes. That's it."

"Then what is all of this? Why is it happening?"

"I don't know, Nino. My friend is dead. My husband was hit and run over by a car, by only God knows who, and someone is watching me…us. Don't you think I want to know too? Don't you think that I'm scared and confused too?"

"I know, baby. I know. I'm just…I'm just worried. About you. About me. That's all."

I didn't reply to him.

Mama Kay didn't say anything.

We rode in silence for the rest of the way to the hotel. Mama Kay checked into a room, on the same floor as ours, and after chatting for a little while, she went her way, and so did we.

"Everything is going to be okay. I'll protect you. Or die trying to," Nino said. "I just wish something started to make sense. Things happening to me and to you is one thing; but then JuJu? Nothing makes sense."

I was numb.

Nino was worried about protecting me, when he was probably the one that needed the protection, because the more and more I thought about it, and even though I wanted to be the blame, I had a feeling that I was wrong.

Maybe it was about Nino.

My husbands' always die.

Only this time, me nor Mama Kay was in control.

At least she wasn't claiming to be.

But if Nino was the one with the target on his back, why kill JuJu?

I was so confused.

"Hold me."

I undressed and though it was mid-afternoon, Nino undressed and climbed into the king-sized hotel bed behind me.

I hadn't really slept in days. I was disappointed in myself for not staying to say my final goodbyes to JuJu, but I wasn't sure if I could handle it, or all of the stares that the other funeral attendees had already started to give me.

"Tighter," I begged him.

I was going to find out who killed JuJu.

Even if I had to beg for Mama Kay's help, someone was going to pay for taking her away from me. And the only form of payment that I would accept, was their death.

Nino held me, in complete silence, and at some time or another, I must've silently cried myself to sleep.

The room was pitch black the next time that I opened my eyes, and with Nino still asleep, I eased out of the bed.

I grabbed my cell phone and headed to use the bathroom.

Sitting on the toilet, I saw that I had roughly 20 notifications, but at that moment, it was only one that stood out. It was only one that mattered.

Days ago, I'd forwarded my work e-mails to my cell phone, and there it was, a new message from the mysterious e-mail address, waiting for me to open it.

I clicked on it, and as usual, the body of the e-mail was empty, but the subject line, this time, mentioned my name…my *real* name.

"Malaysia Christina. It was really nice seeing you today. Black looks good on you."

Ugh!

I growled in frustration, knowing that someone was screwing with me, and it wasn't the least bit okay!

And just before I threw my cell phone at the bathroom wall, I replied; "Okay asshole! Let's play!"

~***~

"Really!"

I screamed from the ground as the mugger ran away with my purse. I'd gotten only a half of a glance of his face.

"Ivy? What happened?"

I heard a voice from behind me, and hurried to sit up. I was wearing a dress, with no panties as usual, and I was sure that he'd just seen an eyeful of my goodies.

Clarke.

Nino's friend.

He was panting, so I could tell that he'd been running to get to me. He took a knee down beside of me.

I was at JuJu's house.

I'd gone by to see if I could go in and get a few things that reminded me of her. I'd checked her secret spot for her house key, but it was gone. It was late in the evening, and after accepting that I wasn't going to be able to get in, I headed back to my car, and that's when the mugger came out of nowhere, grabbed my purse, threw me down, and took off down the street.

"I was just coming by. She must've moved her spare key," I said to him. "And then some asshole, attacked me from behind, and stole my purse."

Clarke helped me to my feet.

After standing up, and making sure that I was properly together, I looked at him, suspiciously.

What the hell was he doing here?

With everything that was going on, Nino was going to go crazy when he found out that I'd gone over there alone. I'd told him that I was going to the store, and I was bummed that now I was going to have to tell him the truth and be forced to listen to one of his lectures.

"What are you doing here, Clarke?"

He didn't answer me at first.

For some reason, I started to feel uneasy.

"Well, she and I…JuJu and I…" he started.

"Yeah. She told me."

"Yeah. We had a thing, but I've been brushing her off lately. I never got to tell her that I was sorry."

"A thing? She said that it was just sex, once, on my wedding night."

Clarke looked confused. "Oh, she did, huh? Your wedding night was the last time that she and I hooked up; but it wasn't the first."

I wondered why JuJu would've lied about it.

"Anyway, this my third time coming by here, since she died. Just to sit and wish that I'd handled things with her differently. I pulled up and saw you on the ground, jumped out of the car and ran to you."

"Did you see the man?"

"What little I could before he cut through those houses." Clarke pointed. "Come on, let's get you to Nino and then to the police."

Since my keys had been inside of my purse, I got into Clarke's car. We didn't speak the whole ride, but I thought about some things that JuJu had said.

She'd said that she couldn't have the man that she wanted because one day he saw me.

She couldn't have been talking about Clarke, right?

No. He and Nino had been friends for years. And he'd been married when I first came into the picture. I wondered when he and JuJu had really started hooking up. Maybe they'd met at our engagement party or something, but I was disappointed that she hadn't been completely honest about them and their situation.

I watched Clarke as he picked up his cell phone. I already knew that he was calling my husband.

He sat for a while, and listened to the ringing on the other end, and then finally, he spoke.

"Hey man, I got your wife…"

~***~

Nino leaned over and threw up in the trash can again.

I rubbed his back and waited for him to finish.

"Come on, get in the bed."

Nino did as he was told, and finally, the doctor came back into the room.

"Mr. Parker, I have your lab results back. And, I'm afraid that I have some bad news."

Nino and I looked at each other in fear.

"It looks as though you have been being poisoned."

"Poisoned?"

"Yes. From the tests that we ran, it looks as though you have been ingesting small amounts, for quite some time now."

Nino looked at me.

"So, what you're saying? Someone has been intentionally poisoning me?"

The doctor looked at me too. "I'm only saying what the reports show. Unless somehow you are eating it on your own, it looks that way. Probably small amounts being put into your drink or in your food. Thankfully, we caught it when we did."

Nino kept his eyes on me.

"I'll give you two a few minutes, to have a discussion, and then we need to get started with your treatment," the doctor said as he left the room.

Nino just sat there. I could tell that he was upset, from the way that he was breathing.

"Are you trying to kill me Ivy?"

"What? No! How could you even ask me something like that?"

"Then explain to me what he just said. I've been out of work for weeks, even before they fired me, so I've only really been around you, every day, well, until here recently, I've been around your mother."

I'll admit, as soon as he'd said poison, I thought of her. Poisoning was a small obsession of hers.

"The doctor said that I was being poisoned, in low dosages, for a while, so you tell me, right fucking now, what's going on Ivy!"

He sudden scream startled me.

After a second, I started to shake my head.

"I swear to you, I don't know. You saw someone in the house that time, remember? Maybe someone is coming in and poisoning our food or drink. Hell, I don't know. You just started throwing up recently. We just went back home a few days ago. At the hotel, you were fine."

"Then why aren't you sick? And he said it's been going on for a while, so that means even before spending what, almost two weeks at the hotel? If it's in our food or drink, at home, why am I the only one sick?"

I shook my head again.

Mama Kay had been gone before JuJu's death, so, if the doctor was sure about his estimation of when the poisoning started, it couldn't have been her.

Someone else was doing this.

To him.

Doing this to me.

Someone was trying to frame me.

"I swear to you, I don't know! I swear! I heard what the doctor said, but it's not me. You're my husband. Why would you even think that it could be me?" I forced myself to cry. Though I was genuinely concerned, I knew that my tears would soften him up, and make what I was saying a little more believable.

For a while, Nino, just sat there and then after listening to me sob for a little while longer, he held out his arms.

"Come here," he instructed me and I sobbed towards him.

"I would never hurt you. I would never hurt anyone," I whined. Nino didn't respond. He just held me close to his heart, probably silently praying that I was telling the truth.

And for the most part, I was.

****

Chapter FOUR

"I'm sorry for your loss," Cage finally had a chance to speak to me, while I was alone, and since we'd been back at the house.

We were packing.

I'd spent almost a week trying to convince Nino, that it had to be someone else poisoning him, and possibly trying to kill him. He considered all of the other things that had been going on, and seemed to believe me. Once he was out of the hospital, we got on the ball with finding a new house.

Quickly, we decided on a home, closed on it, and we were finally packing, hoping to be moved by the end next week.

Things had been quiet lately.

Nothing strange had happened. No e-mails had come. Other than finding out that Nino had been poisoned, and the stress and awkwardness that came along with that, everything had been okay.

I'd asked Mama Kay if she'd poisoned Nino, just to be sure, and she laughed at me. She'd simply said, that if she'd done it, she wouldn't have gotten caught, Nino wouldn't have lived, and that he nor the doctor would've ever known.

I believed her.

Then she told me more about the poison that the doctor had found in Nino's system and she confirmed, in front of him, that the type of poison, and in small amounts, could take quite some time to take effect. It causes a lot of sickness with it, making it obvious that someone is intentionally doing it. She told him that he could've encountered it, for the first time, weeks ago, and he would've never even known it.

Her comments helped my case with Nino.

But it didn't help hers.

She could've been being sloppy on purpose, just to throw me off. I couldn't deny that Nino thought that he'd seen her when a truck almost hit him a while ago, though, Mama Kay seemed to be in a different space.

But I couldn't be sure. I couldn't be sure of anything except that someone wanted my 13th husband dead.

"Thank you. I never got a chance to thank you, for that day."

It had been weeks since JuJu's death, and the news had moved on from her story. But I hadn't forgotten her.

The day that she'd been shot, once I started to scream, the entire neighborhood came outside to see what was going on. Cage was the only one that ran over to help.

He'd tried to save her.

He performed CPR, and pumped her chest, but he couldn't. He couldn't bring her back no matter how hard he tried.

"No problem." Cage turned to walk away.

"Um, I was actually going to come over and ask you if I could borrow some tape. I've been packing all day and we're out."

"Oh, you're moving?"

"Yeah. After the shooting, there's no way that I can stay here." Cage nodded with understanding. "Anyway, I was mugged not too long ago, and I'm still uncomfortable with going anywhere alone. Nino's at a doctor's appointment, and my Mama is in the house taking a nap. So, I don't want to go by myself. But if you don't have any, that's fine. I'll just call Nino and have him pick some up after---,"

"No worries. I have some."

He led the way and I followed him.

Though we'd shared plenty of intimate moments in the past, they were always outside, or inside of my house. I'd never actually been inside of his.

We walked up his front steps and the surprising scent of cinnamon tingled the hairs inside of my nose.

Stepping inside, it was nothing like I'd thought it would be.

It was clean.

Not the bachelor pad set up that I was expecting. Everything was in its place, and it smelled good too.

I followed him into the kitchen.

The counters were so clean that you could eat off of them and all of his dishes were washed and placed neatly in the drain.

"If only I could get my husband to be as clean as you are," I giggled.

Cage chuckled.

"Old habits, die hard. I was a military brat. My dad served for years. And you know how that goes. Everything was always clean. Everything was always in order."

Cage opened and shut a few drawers as I inched behind him. I stopped to admire the cookbook that he had on the counter. I noticed that he had red check marks on some of the pages.

"Don't tell me that you cook too?"

"I create. It's a difference," he laughed.

"You clean and cook? Where have you been all of my life?" I joked.

"Right next door," he said softly.

His comment made the next few seconds between us slightly awkward. Needing to get by me, he slightly brushed up against me, and a chill shot down my spine.

My eyes closed instinctively, as the result of the strong, arousing aroma of his skin and my knees started to buckle without my consent.

I turned around to face him.

"Here you go," he said, reaching me the roll of tape.

He waited for me to take it from his hands, but for some reason, I couldn't. I couldn't move.

"Ivy?"

"Huh?"

"Tape."

I looked past the tape and into his eyes. There was so much warmth inside of them. So much tenderness. So much desire. He wanted me, just as much as I wanted him. I could see it. I could feel it.

With all that had been going on, of course Nino and I hadn't gotten busy in between the sheets, in what seemed like forever. I hadn't been complaining, or even in the mood, but Cage, his presence, his...everything, made it hard to keep sex off of my mind.

We both breathed hard.

It was as though someone had sucked all of the air out of the room.

Take the tape and leave, Ivy.

I coached myself to do the right thing, yet I inched closer to Cage. When he didn't move, I knew that he was feeling the same way that I was. I felt as though we were on the same page, and before I could stop myself…

I kissed him.

It took him a second, but eventually, Cage dropped the tape, and pulled me closer to him. Finally, he started to kiss me back. Our lips intertwined, sending me into something like a daze.

I was intoxicated by him and from the feeling that his lips and tongue supplied. His kisses took me higher and higher. I was so high, that I never wanted to come down.

But Cage left me no choice.

Hurriedly, he pulled himself away from me.

"What? What's wrong?"

He wiped the corners of his mouth, and took a deep breath. "I'm sorry. I don't *do* married women," he confessed, reminding me that I belonged to someone else.

I stared at him.

Apart of me was hoping that he would change his mind.

I wasn't sure why. I'd never had an affair before, and had always stayed true to my vows, but internally, I pouted and cursed him for having self-control.

Maybe it was because of the lack of sex or because there was so much space in between Nino and I. Or maybe it was because of everything that had been going on, and I just wanted something to make me feel good. Hell, or maybe it was just because it was him. Whatever it was, I still wanted him. And I wanted him to want me too.

After a while of just standing there, in embarrassment, I bent over to pick up to roll of tape.

"Um, I guess, thanks for the tape," I said to him.

"No problem."

He followed me towards the front door. I was extremely disappointed, but there was still lust and desire soaring through the air.

I could feel it and I knew that he had to feel it too.

"Um, so I guess, with the move and all, this is goodbye," I said to him, turning around just as I reached the front door.

He smiled at me, and then his eyes wandered down to the floor. He tucked his head full of curls behind his ears, and I literally had to keep myself from pouncing on him.

"Okay. Bye." I said, grabbing the door knob, to the front door, lingering, hoping that he would say something, but he didn't.

I exhaled loudly, but just as I opened the door, I felt Cage walk closer to me. And then I saw his hand, reach up and push the front door close. He still didn't say anything as he ran his hands down the sides of my body.

I shuddered at his touch, and once he kissed the back of my neck, I knew that he was going to give me what I wanted, so I dropped the tape and turned around to face him.

Mentally, I felt a small amount of wrong and conviction, but emotionally, physically, and sexually, I was all in! Somehow, there was satisfaction in my heart, knowing that I would no longer have to imagine how Cage would feel inside of me.

Now, I would have a memory.

~***~

"I like the new house."

I read the e-mail aloud.

Our house was in the heart of a cul-de-sac, but still, I looked around.

I didn't see anyone. I didn't see a car that was out of place. I didn't see a random person behind a tree or a row of bushes. I didn't see anything.

"Ivy? Are you okay?"

Nino stopped in front of me, carrying a box.

"We're safe here. Everything has been fine. There's nothing to worry about."

Nino headed inside, as I glanced at the e-mail again.

"Safe my ass," I mumbled.

Nothing weird had happened since the mugging and the discovery of Nino's poisoning. No one had tried to use my credit cards or anything. I'd replaced them, my cell phone, my keys, and everything without a hitch. Nino's life hadn't been threatened, and for a little while, things were starting to feel normal again.

But today, the same day that we were moving into our new house, the strange e-mails, decided to roll in.

I headed inside, hurriedly, closing and locking the door behind me.

I spotted Mama Kay hanging photos on the wall.

"You should go home to your husband," I whispered to her.

"He understands."

"There isn't that much understanding in the world," I replied, as she continued with her task and then she started to hum.

"What is that song?"

"You've only heard it a thousand times since you were little," she said to me.

"I know. But what song is it?"

"It's a song that I learned from my mother. Never really knew the name of it. Maybe she'd made it up," she said, sadly.

"Do you ever miss her? My grandmother? Do you ever think about her or your sister that you left behind? Do you think that grandma is still alive?"

"I doubt it. If so, she's old as dirt, don't you think?" She giggled. "And no. I don't miss them. All I care about is you."

And with that, she moved to the next wall and proceeded with humming her tune.

I headed to find Nino.

"Hello beautiful, I guess you don't plan to do a damn thing today huh," Nino joked.

He and I were still in a strange place.

He always seemed so worried about everything; about me, and especially about himself. I couldn't blame him though. I would be worried too after all that he'd gone through lately.

Yet, I could tell that he was trying.

He was trying to see some good, even after all of the bad that had happened. Even when there were things that he didn't understand.

We'd finally had sex, twice, last week, but it was nothing like sex used to be between us. He wasn't weird, or rough or even as attentive to my body as he was prior to the incidents, but I could only hope that in due time, if nothing else happened, that things between us would go back to the way that they were.

I wasn't complaining though, because whenever I wanted "more" I would take a nice long bath, and please myself to the memories of sex with Cage.

I found it hard to feel bad about something that had felt so good. That day, Cage had taken his time with me, pleased me beyond my wildest dreams and ten times better than in my imagination. Though I vowed to never step out on my marriage again, physically, mentally, these days, I cheated on Nino all the time.

"Once we get settled, you need to get that business started," I told him.

"I will, but that's the last thing on my mind."

"Then what is on your mind?"

He didn't reply.

"Tell me. I know you are pretending that everything is okay, for me, but I would love it if you would actually talk to me," I walked closer to him.

Nino exhaled. "I'm fine. Really. I just want to make sure that you are safe. That we are safe. I wouldn't feel comfortable just yet, leaving you for hours, if I didn't have to, trying to get a business off the ground, not knowing if something else out of the blue was going to happen."

"We're safe here, remember? That's what you just said." I smiled at him, even though I knew that someone was still watching us.

I'd been working from home, for weeks now, so that Nino would feel comfortable, but just waiting around for something else crazy or unexpected to take place, wasn't doing any of us any good.

Nino touched the side of my face.

He leaned in to kiss me, but Mama Kay's sudden scream, caused us both to jump and then take off running.

We found her in the living room, standing by the window.

"What is it Mama?"

"I was about to hang up a picture, and I looked up to see some fool in a ski-mask, staring back at me," she said, moving closer to the window, as Nino headed towards the front door. "It caught me off guard. Scared the Jesus, and just a little bit of piss right on out of me," she shared too much information.

I saw Nino come back in, and go for the box where he kept his gun.

"I don't see anyone. Did you see where he went?"

"He? Who said that it was a he? That was a she."

Nino and I both looked at each other.

"A she? A woman? In a mask? Are you sure?"

Mama Kay placed her hands on her hip. "As old as I am, I'm pretty sure that I can tell a man from a woman. It was a she," she said and she walked out of the living room.

A she?

Now, I was even more confused.

~*** ~

"Nice to have you back," my boss Jarret said.

I hadn't been into work for a long while, since the day before JuJu died. A part of me wanted to just let the job go. I didn't really need to work anyway, but there I was, sitting behind my desk, pretending to be somewhere that I didn't want to be.

"We left her office, just the way that she left it. No one has been in there. I know how close the two of you were, so I wanted to let you be the one to clear out her things. No rush. Well, except that her replacement will start in two weeks. If possible, could you have it cleared out by then?"

I nodded.

It wasn't until that moment that I decided that once I cleared out her things, I was clearing out mine too.

It just wasn't going to be the same without her there.

I headed to JuJu's office.

Immediately, I noticed that she didn't have much in there. Her office seemed quite empty. I looked through her desk drawers. There was nothing important there; actually, there was nothing there at all. Her drawers were clear; clean, as though she'd been planning to quit or something before she died.

She had one coffee mug, and photo of herself in the Bahamas on her desk, and that was it.

Literally.

Her closet was empty. The shelves only had things that pertained to work, and all of her personal items that had been there before, were gone.

Where was she going?

Had she been planning to quit without telling me?

I sat back down in front of her desk and turned on her computer. I tried to guess her password and when I couldn't, I grabbed her mug and her photo and I headed for the door. Glancing at the mug, suddenly, I thought about something that she always used to say.

"JuJu 2.0."

She always said that when she was giving herself a pep talk. She would say that she needed JuJu 2.0. to show up, and show out, especially when she was tired, or wasn't doing as good of a job as she knew that she could.

I sat the mug and picture on the shelf by the door and headed back to her computer. In the password space, I typed in JuJu2.0 and, wah-lah, it worked!

I was in.

I scrolled through everything, but just like her desk and shelves, everything was pretty much wiped clean…except for a few photos that were hiding in her recycle bin.

She must've forgotten to permanently delete them.

I recovered the three photos that were there and looked at them closely. Imagine my surprise to find that all of them…were of me.

One of them was while I was at work.

We were in my office. It was taken while I didn't seem to be paying any attention to her. Another one was on my wedding day. I remembered the exact moment.

Nino and I had just cut the cake, and after eating my piece, I turned around to smile at Mama. She'd captured that very moment. And the last picture was of me, getting into the ambulance, the day that Nino was ran over. It was only of the back of me, just before they shut the ambulance door.

That picture made me uncomfortable.

Why would she take a picture of me that day?

Why had she taken any of them at all?

I was still receiving the e-mails, and since she was dead, I knew those weren't from her, but why would she have been secretly taking random pictures of me?

She'd been there when Nino was run down by the car and of course, she hadn't been the one to do it. But what if she'd known that it was going to happen?

Seeing the pictures made me wonder if she'd really been there by coincidence.

I mean, the pictures had to mean something…right?

Or maybe they didn't mean anything bad at all.

I'd known JuJu to have a thing or two with another woman before. Maybe she'd had a thing for me, and just didn't show it. Maybe she'd just done a hell of a good job at hiding it.

And now she was dead, so no matter what the pictures meant, I couldn't ask her.

Deleting them, and after making sure that there wasn't anything else on her computer, I grabbed the only two items she'd left behind, and I headed back to my office to gather my things.

After calling Jarret into my office, and telling him that I was sorry, but I had to go, he almost went insane! He offered me everything but a Rolls Royce to stay, but once I declined, he said that the last few weeks had been hell for me and that he understood.

I knew that Nino wouldn't mind that fact that I'd quit. He'd begged me to stay home that morning anyway. And now that I would no longer be working, I could simply assist him with getting his business started, and if I ever needed to go in my stash, I would just lie on Mama Kay again.

Somewhat feeling better about my decision, once I was outside, I smiled once I placed the things into my car and then got inside.

Ding.

I already knew what the sound meant before I looked at my cell phone.

I opened the e-mail.

"Where are you going?"

The subject line read.

I sat my cell phone in the passenger seat, but immediately, it dinged again.

"I love it when you wear red."

I glanced down at my red blouse, and frowned knowing that whoever was stalking me, was somewhere close by.

I concluded that whoever the e-mails were coming from, they didn't want to hurt me. If they wanted to, they would've done so already. They were always near, they were always watching, maybe they just wanted my attention. They seemed to know my every move. They knew my real name, and I couldn't be sure as to what else they knew about me or my past, but I was tired of playing their little game.

If they wanted me, they knew where to find me.

And with that in mind, I didn't reply to the e-mails. Instead, I deleted my work e-mail account from my phone, since I no longer needed it anymore, anyway, and I threw the phone back into the passenger seat and drove away.

Cage and I stared at each other from across the store.

As soon as I'd walked in, I'd spotted him, and after a while, finally, he saw me.

We just stared at each other.

I figured that neither of us knew what to say.

We hadn't spoken since the day that we'd had sex. We would just stare at each other in passing, but neither of us would say a word.

I walked closer, and I thought that we were just going to pass by each other but, he stopped.

"Hey Ivy."

"Hey Cage."

We continued to look at each other, and I could feel myself, starting to sweat. I almost felt nervous from being in his presence and I wasn't sure why.

Cage on the other hand, looked at me with thirst.

"I can't keep you off of my mind, since that day," Cage blurted out. My heart skipped a beat. "I think about you all the time, even though I know I shouldn't."

The butterflies in my stomach started to flutter. I was surprised at his words, since he'd always been a little shy. I smiled and him, and just as I was about to reply, he changed the subject. "Um, so how's everything. You know, with you? And the move? And all?"

Thrown for a loop, I responded.

"Good. Everything is good."

"That's good. That's real good."

Both of us grew silent. Just as I was about to speak, yet again, he cut me off.

"Someone has moved in over there already, in your old house," he said.

"Really?"

"Yes. But she isn't as pretty as you," he slipped out, just as a woman approached him.

"Baby, is this it?" She held up a can.

She noticed me watching her and after seeing that Cage wasn't going to introduce her, she introduced herself.

"Hey. I'm Sheree."

"Hey. Sheree. I'm Ivy."

"Oh. The woman who moved out of the house that I moved into."

I glanced at Cage, who somewhat seemed as though he wanted to laugh, but I wasn't sure why.

And he'd lied.

She was drop-dead gorgeous!

Admitting that another woman was more attractive than you were, was never easy, but she was. Hell, if I was a man, or into women, I'd want to lick her and maybe even drink her bath water. Seriously, she was one of the prettiest women that I'd ever seen.

"Nice to meet you. Cage, nice seeing you again," I said, and just as she snuggled close to him, and locked her arm into his, I turned to walk away.

For some reason, my body was on fire with jealousy.

I was married, and even though we'd shared something so wonderful and amazing, I still belonged to someone else, and apparently, now, so did he. But that didn't stop me from feeling the way that I did.

For the rest of the time in the store, I found myself, continuously glancing in their direction. I watched how she flirted with him, and as she hugged all over him. I watched how he smiled at her and held her hand. Finally, I watched them head towards the door to leave.

My feelings were slightly hurt, as I watched Cage hold the door open for her, and for some reason, I waited to see if he would glance back at me.

He did.

~***~

"I'll sit this one out," I said to Nino, as we pulled up in front of another building. He was out looking at locations for his new CPA business. Once I saw him shake hands with the Realtor of the building, I turned my attention back to my phone.

I was planning a romantic getaway for Nino and I. After all we'd been going through, we needed it; especially since he would be focusing on his new business soon. But more importantly, we needed to rekindle some old flames. Things still weren't the same between us, and being that I couldn't get Cage off of my mind, I needed this trip.

We needed this trip.

I searched for flights on my phone for a while, and then I noticed the black car, pull up behind us.

The windows were tinted, dark, and I waited to see who would get out of it, but no one ever did.

All of a sudden, and maybe it was because of the tinted windows that were so dark that you couldn't see who was driving, but the car caused me to think about Nino's hit and run incident. It wasn't the same color as the car from the accident, but thinking about that night that someone was creeping around at our old house, it could've been the same car that I'd seen back then.

I didn't trust it.

I locked the car doors.

I stared at the car, continuously, and just as I was about to call Nino, he came out of the building.

Suddenly, the car sped off down the road, faster than a speeding bullet. Way too fast for me to try and get the license plate number.

I unlocked the car doors, for Nino to get inside. He locked the doors back, once he was in his seat.

Still wondering about the black car, finally, I looked at Nino. His face was full of concern as he looked in the same direction as the car had gone.

"Did you like it?"

Nino didn't say anything.

"What? Was it that bad?"

"I can't get this one."

"What? Why?"

I watched the Realtor come out of the building and walk down the street until he was out of sight.

"Nino, I'm confused. What did he say?"

"I don't know what the fuck is going on!"

"What? Nino, talk to me, damn it!"

"When I got inside, he told me that I wouldn't be able to buy the building. He said that the man that he'd just met, before me, had purchased it. I was pissed that he didn't call and tell me that before we got here, but I thanked him, and turned to leave. Then he said, that the man, told him to give me a message. I thought he was on some bullshit, until he started talking."

My stomach turned into knots as I awaited his next words.

"He said to tell me that the woman that I love, isn't who she says that she is. That I was in danger every day that I was with her. And then he told me to ask you about Malaysia. At first, I didn't know how to take it and then he said: Ask Ivy about Malaysia. Who is Malaysia, Ivy?"

My face tensed as Nino looked at me.

I'd looked directly at the Realtor as he'd walked away. I knew that I'd never met him before. I didn't know who he was and there was no way that he knew me, but whoever he'd met up with, before Nino...knew me, and obviously, they knew me well.

And I wanted to know who it was.

Now!

"Malaysia?" I asked, trying to think of a lie.

"Malaysia?" Nino repeated my question.

I wasn't sure who was playing games with me, my husband and my marriage, but I didn't like it.

I didn't like it one bit.

"Ivy? Say something. Why would he say that you aren't who you say that you are? And that I'm in danger as long as I'm with you? Who is Malaysia?"

I knew that I had to tell him something, but too much might be bad for me. If I told him that I changed my name, he would have tons of questions, that I would refuse to answer. But I had to make whatever I said believable; which meant that I was going to have to tell him just a little bit of the truth; mostly lies, but just a tad bit of the truth.

Oh well. Here goes nothing.

"Malaysia is a *where*...not a *who*. I was married before...to a man that I'd met in Malaysia, a few years ago. We'd met there, at an expansion meeting with a company that I used to work for. He lived in the states though."

Nino knew that I'd done some traveling before, so I was hoping that it didn't sound too farfetched.

Nino looked at me with the stink face. "I thought you said that you had never been married before."

"I lied."

"Why Ivy? Why?"

"Because...he died."

~***~

"I'm not going anywhere until you pee on this stick," Mama Kay said.

Honestly, I didn't need to pee to confirm what I already knew. Though I'd never been pregnant before, I had all of the signs.

I was pregnant.

Finally, I was going to have a baby!

If only it was the right time.

After talking to Nino that day, he acted as though he was married to a killer!

The fact that I'd lied about being married, was one thing, but not telling him that my ex-husband was dead, was another! I could only imagine what he would do or say if he knew that the total count of dead husbands in my past was twelve. He would probably haul ass and never look back.

Now, without him saying it, I knew that in his mind, he was positive that I'd been trying to kill him.

Though I'd tried to tell him that the fake dead husband, that I'd met on a fake international business trip, had died by accident, he didn't believe me...especially since I wouldn't give him his name.

I was sure that I was making things worse for myself, but I just couldn't tell him the truth. Not about me, not about my husbands, and damn sure not about my Mama.

Now, Nino pretty much stayed the hell away from me. He slept on the couch and he was barely saying a word to me, no matter how much I tried to explain.

I'd asked him if he wanted a divorce, and he wouldn't even answer the question. He just walked around looking at me crazy all damn day.

"Take the test."

"I don't need a test, Mama."

"Yes, you do. Take it."

I took the test from her hands and headed to the bathroom.

Mama Kay could sense that something was wrong between Nino and I, but she never asked and I hadn't taken the time to try and explain.

"Hurry up," she knocked as soon as she heard me start to pee. "Come on. Bring it out."

I flushed the toilet, washed my hands, and brought the test out to her. She watched it, waiting on the answer, and once I saw her smile, I knew that it was confirmed.

"Pregnant!" Mama Kay beamed.

I just stood there, in shock and worry.

I'd imagined that I would be the happiest woman in the world when I finally got pregnant, but I wasn't.

And I was about to tell Mama Kay why.

"You're finally going to be a mother! This is what you've always wanted," she said as she studied my face. "But I guess you assumed that when it happened you would know who the father is."

I looked at her in a hurry as she folded her arms over her chest.

Oh shit! I hadn't even thought about that!

Not only was I worried about what was going on with my marriage, but it had slipped my mind that I'd slept with Cage!

"What? You thought that I didn't know? You were in there with him for a long while, that day. That fine ass neighbor of yours. I'm not a fool, daughter."

"I thought---,"

"What? That I was asleep? Yeah. I bet you did. Honey, you should know by now, that I don't miss anything, especially when it comes to you."

I rolled my eyes.

Now, I could add something else to stress about to the list. Convincing Nino that I wasn't trying to kill him, and trying to beg him to forgive me for the lie, that was yet another lie, was already an emotional workout.

And now, possibly being pregnant by another man...yeah, I was about to be stressed out to the max! Then again, maybe not, because there was no way in hell that I was telling him about Cage!

"Are you going to tell him?" Mama Kay asked, and I let out a chuckle.

"Nope. I've lied about worse."

"Haven't we all. And judging by the way both of you have been walking around here lately, how much does he know?"

Damn! Was she psychic?

"Not much. I got it."

"I know you do, daughter. Then it's settled. You and your husband are having a baby. I suggest you work on your facial expression, and pull some kind of fake happiness out of your ass, before you tell him. You look more like a woman who just found out that she had a STD, versus a woman who has waited all of her life to hear that she was pregnant," Mama Kay stated, and then she told me that she was going to fly home, to her own husband, for a few days to give us some space to work things out and allow me to break the news to Nino.

Apart of me didn't want her to leave, but I didn't tell her that and over the next few days, Mama Kay made her way back to Louisiana, and I made my way to the doctor, alone.

"I'll be back," I'd said to Nino.

He hadn't asked where I was going, or when I would be back. He hadn't said anything. He just nodded his head as though he no longer cared about protecting me, or making sure that I was safe.

"You aren't that far along, but you are absolutely pregnant! Look, right there," my doctor said as she moved the instrument around in my vagina.

I wanted to cry, but I didn't.

This moment should've been shared with my husband. And there I was. Alone. Unsure of what to do next.

After a few more things, I headed out of the doctor's office, and as I approached the car, I could see that all of my tires were flat. All four of them were on their rims.

"Ugh! Not today," I huffed.

No one was lingering around, even though I knew that my stalker, was somewhere close by.

I debated on whether calling Nino was a good idea. Mad or not, I knew that he would come, but then I would have to explain why I was there.

Then again, I'd planned on telling him the news once I got back home anyway, so I guess it wasn't that big of a deal.

I called him, and after the fourth call, he finally answered his phone.

"Nino. I need you to come and pick me up. Someone let the air out of all of my tires."

Surprisingly, he seemed concerned. I told him where I was and he was there in less than five minutes.

After figuring out what he wanted to do with my car, we called a tow truck. Once they picked it up, we got into his car and we drove towards home. He didn't say anything or ask me why I'd gone to see the doctor.

Once we arrived home, I wondered if telling him that I was pregnant, would make things better between us.

Maybe it would make him see that we were worth fighting for. And I hoped that the tire incident, further confirmed for him that someone was messing with both of us, but I wasn't sure if he would see it that way.

I'd forced him to reach back out to the Realtor, to try to get a name out of him, but the Realtor's phone number had been disconnected.

He had to see how all of this looked, and that someone was just causing trouble, even if some of the things that they were saying were true.

Someone was screwing with me, and messing everything up! But according to Nino, when I hadn't told him the truth, I'd messed us up from the very beginning.

I was praying that this baby made everything better.

As far as Cage was concerned, I planned to never tell him about the baby. If I ran into him, while I was pregnant, I wouldn't hesitate to say that the baby was my husband's. After all, it could be.

Nino walked into the kitchen.

"I just put in offer in on a building. We will see how it goes."

I forced a smile. He didn't.

"I'm making your favorite tonight. Fish stew."

"Oh."

I stopped what I was doing, and I grabbed him by the hand.

"We need to talk."

"About what? Is there something else that you need to tell me?" Nino said.

"Actually, there is. I'm…we're…going to have a baby! I'm pregnant!" I squealed, trying to show excitement, hoping that he would too, but Nino looked as though he was constipated.

I was hoping that the news softened him up just a little, and that it would be motivation for us to start working out our issues, but he was giving me a totally different vibe.

"Did you hear me? That's why I was at the doctor's office today. I'm pregnant. Hold on, I have the confirmation ultrasound, and---."

"Who's the father, Ivy?"

I froze.

What the hell?

Why would he ask me that?

What did he know?

I turned to face him.

"So, let me get this straight. You lied about being married before. He's dead, and you won't tell me the man's name. And now, I find out that you were cheating on me, too? And you didn't have the decency to use protection? Who in the hell did I get married to?"

"What? No. What are you talking about? Of course, not! The baby is yours Nino!"

That was my story, and unless he had some kind of proof, I was sticking to it!

I started to sweat.

"No. It isn't. So, whose baby, is it? Who have you been sleeping with, Ivy? Don't you think that I deserve the truth?"

I could tell by the look on his face that he was serious, but I wouldn't let that break me. I slammed the ultrasound down on the counter.

"I don't know where all of this is coming from! I don't know why you would be asking me something like this! I don't know who is screwing with me and putting all of these things in your head about me! But you ARE my husband and this IS your baby!" I yelled at him, but Nino shook his head.

"No. It isn't Ivy. And I know for a fact that it's not mine because…I can't have kids." Nino revealed and my mouth dropped open. "I can't have kids…at all," he confirmed. "Now do you want to tell me who the father is?"

Wait a minute…what did he just say?

****

Chapter FIVE

"Are you going to leave me?"

Nino looked at me. "Nope. We both lied. I guess now we're even," And with that, Nino was gone.

The night that I revealed to him that I was pregnant, he dropped a bomb on me, confessing that he couldn't have kids, due to having a vasectomy, years before I'd even come into the picture.

Therefore, he knew that the baby wasn't his.

He'd told me that before me, that before us, he'd never wanted kids. He'd said that he was sure of it, until he met me and that all I talked about was a husband and kids. He'd said that he hadn't wanted to disappoint me by telling me his truth, so instead, he'd figured that once we tried for a while, and once I didn't get pregnant, that he would just suggest adoption.

He thought that he had it all figured out.

Until, I told him that I was pregnant.

I'd even had the nerve to get upset at the fact that he'd lied to me, but he pointed out all of my lies, and shut down my blame game immediately.

He asked me who I'd been sleeping with, and I admitted that it only happened once; which it did. That was the truth. But I lied and told him that it was with a man that I worked with, which I used that as another excuse of why I quit my job.

Yes. I was tired of lying, but I promised myself, that this baby lie was the last one.

I told him that we weren't having sex and that I was emotional about JuJu and that it was something that just happened. I told him that it didn't mean anything and that it would never happen again.

I didn't tell him that I'd had sex with Cage, only because I didn't want any more trouble than there already was. I didn't want to cause any more problems, and because Nino knew exactly who he was and where to find him, I felt that lying about the father of my baby was what was best.

Yet, that day, we ended the conversation quickly.

We walked around for days, not saying one single word to each other, until the night before.

Nino approached me in the kitchen and touched my stomach. He asked a few questions about the baby and how I was feeling and that was it.

I walked over to the window, to watch him drive away.

He was still there, so that had to count for something.

I had been going crazy trying to figure out what was going on. Mama Kay was pulling every string that she could after I finally told her what the Realtor had said to Nino.

Someone knew about my past, and someone was trying to turn Nino against me. I was waiting for Mama Kay to suggest killing Nino, and simply moving away with the baby, but she never did, confirming for me that she was keeping her promise to me, and trying to find other solutions.

I saw the delivery truck stop in front of our house.

I watched the man as he walked towards the front door.

"Yes. Ms. Katie Graham."

"That's my mother. Can I sign for her?"

He nodded.

I signed and took the small, thin, rectangular box from his hands. It was as light as a feather, and after thanking him, I headed inside to call Mama Kay.

"Hey Mama, a package came for you."

"For me?"

"Yes. It's addressed to you. You want me to open it and see what it is?" I shook the package to try to hear what was inside of it.

"No. I'll be there at the end of the week. And I think I found something."

At her words, I sat the package on the table and took a seat. I waited for her to say something, but she never did. At least not about the matters at hand.

"When I come at the end of the week, I plan to stay," Mama Kay said.

"What? What about Simeon, Mama? What about your husband?"

She waited for a long while and then finally she said.

"What husband?"

I froze at her words.

Uh Oh.

~***~

"How could you be so stupid? Driving drunk Nino? Really? And since when do you get drunk?"

I chastised him as we walked into the house.

I'd received a phone call from him, at 3 a.m. saying that he was in jail for a DUI.

Nino wobbled in my direction. He'd had some time to sleep it off, but I could tell that he was still intoxicated.

"You could've hurt someone. Or yourself! You could've gotten yourself killed!" I screamed at him as I plopped down on the couch.

"You're already trying to kill me, what's the difference?"

I scowled at him, and he looked at me as though he was trying to read my mind.

"You really aren't trying to kill me, are you?

"No, dumb ass! I'm not. And I've told you that a thousand times! I lied about being married before. And I've told you over and over again that my ex-husband died by accident. So, no, I'm not trying to kill you! I love you!" I blurted at him, as he fell onto the couch beside of me, and I couldn't believe that he rested his head on my lap.

"Which husband did you love the most?" Nino slurred.

I froze. I was confused by the question.

Had I heard him correctly?

"What did you say?"

"Which husband was your favorite?"

I could tell that he was falling asleep, but still, he continued to speak.

"Hello? I said, out of *all* your husbands, which…one…did…" Nino started to snore, and immediately, I moved him off of me.

All?

He'd said all!

What was going on here?

He knew about *all* of my husbands?

He knew the truth about me?

All damn sure meant more than two!

Did he know about my past?

How?

Fear surrounded me, and I tried to steady my heartbeat.

If he knew the truth about my husbands, then what else did Nino know about me?

~***~

Mama Kay had been silent since we left the airport.

And so was I.

Nino's comments had been the only thing on my mind. He'd asked which husband was my favorite. I'd heard it with my own two ears.

I was sure that he hadn't known before. Not after the way that he'd flipped out when finding out that I'd been married to someone else, before him.

Someone had told him something.

Someone knew.

I opened my mouth fill Mama Kay in, but she beat me to the punch.

"Simeon…"

I glanced at her.

"Oh no, Mama. Tell me that you didn't kill him."

"I didn't. I couldn't…because he's working with the police."

I slammed on my brakes, and a car wailed its horn behind me.

"Drive Daughter," she said. I cleared my throat and did as I was told. "He's been working with them the whole time. I was never around. It was easy to miss. The day that I left, to give you guys some space, I hadn't told him that I was coming back home. I was going to surprise him. When I got there, he wasn't there. I was going to call him, but as I started to look around, I could tell that he'd been going through my things. And then on the coffee table, there was an obituary of his son…and wedding photos of you and husbands #9 through #13."

A chill came out of nowhere, and slapped me in the face. I'd always heard that no matter what you're hiding, the truth always finds its way to the light. But things coming to the light about my past marriages could be really bad…for both of us.

"My mind went into overdrive, but you know your Mama, I had to play it smart. I left, as though I'd never gone home. I texted him and told him that I would be there soon, and wasted hours gambling nearby. By the time that I got back home, everything was back in its proper place. My things were neat, as though they'd never been touched, and the obituary and photos were out of sight."

I took in everything that she'd said.

"Maybe...maybe there's an explanation for all of this."

She chuckled.

"They are building a case on you," she said and looked me directly into my eyes. "They that think you are a murderer. They think that you had all of your dead husbands killed. They think that you were the mastermind behind them all."

I shook my head no.

"After seeing the photos, I acted normal with Simeon, but I started to do things that I wouldn't normally do. I started saying random things, about you, and one night, I caught him recording me. He'd even had the nerve to ask me to repeat myself, not knowing that I'd watched him click the record voice memo button on his cell phone. I have never, not even once, called you "Ivy" in front of him, since he knows you as Malaysia. I'm careful to always call you "Daughter" when speaking of you, to him, or to you, around him, but one day, he almost called you Ivy. He stopped himself and I pretended not to notice. So, tell me, if I've never called you by that name, how would he know that you go by Ivy? And I promise you, I know for a fact that I've never said it. And then there was one night, he told me that he was going to a bar with a few of his poker buddies. I followed him. Indeed, he drove to the bar, but he got into a black car that was waiting for him in the parking lot; black with dark tinted windows."

"I've seen a car like that around here too," I confessed to her.

"They sat in the car for a long while. And then Simeon got out of the car, went into the bar alone, and the car drove away. I gave the license plate to a friend…it's registered to the Virginia Police Department. Of course, the tag looked as though it was a civilian tag, but still, it was registered by the law."

I exhaled.

"Now mind you, driving from Virginia to Louisiana, is a hell of a drive, but it can be done; especially if you think you're on to something. We tend to go above and beyond when we're working undercover. And if they're in Virginia, I'm referring to the police, then that only tells me that it's you who they are watching. It's you who they are after."

My mouth was extremely dry, and I didn't know what to say. All I could seem to think about was the past, the future…and my unborn child.

"Simeon approached me on that cruise ship on purpose. He thinks that you killed his son. And he's trying to prove it. And he didn't care if he had to get close to me to do it."

"But I didn't kill his son."

"And technically, neither did I."

"Who did then? Who helps you, Mama?"

"I told you, that's something I'll never tell you. Those favors are between me and them. Besides, they'll never find anything. But they are looking. I see things clearer now. This whole time, Simeon has wanted me to lead him to you. He would complain as to why he had to be a secret. And then once I told him that you knew about us, he begged me to invite you around. He's even planning to sell his auto shop soon, and asked me if I wanted us to move here, so that I could be closer to you. He told me that he just wanted to make things easy for me and make me happy. It was all a lie. I'm disappointed in myself, because I should've seen it a long time ago."

If Mama Kay was right, I wasn't sure what it all meant for me. I was innocent; literally. I'd never actually killed anyone, so I wanted to say that there was no need for me to worry, but I would be a fool to think that someway, somehow, that this couldn't turn out badly for me.

"And it makes me wonder if all of the strange things going on, is somehow connected to Simeon. What if he's been trying to frame you? All of this time? What if he has been behind the incidents with Nino, hoping to give the police something to go on, to get to you? What if he's been sending you the e-mails? Or behind what happened to your friend? No one would've ever suspected him. At least now we're ahead of it all."

She didn't say anything else for a long while, and neither did I. Once we arrived at my house, just as we opened the car doors, finally, she said a few last words.

"Don't worry. As always, I'll protect you."

I knew that she meant it; but what would she have to do, to do it?

~***~

"Nino, the other night, you said something," I mentioned to him.

Now that I knew that Simeon was up to something, I couldn't go around pretending as though I hadn't heard him. I needed to know what he knew.

"You said---."

"I know what I said Ivy," Nino replied, repeating what he'd said that night, word for word, and then he headed to our bedroom closet. He pulled out a small, thin, package, one that was identical to the one that Mama Kay had received in the mail some time ago, only this one was addressed to him.

"Open it."

I opened the package.

"I received it not too long ago," Nino said, as he watched me go through each photo.

It was wedding pictures, of me, with EVERY, SINGLE, HUSBAND!

Literally, it was 13 wedding photos, even one of Nino and I. Ours wasn't a professional one, it had been taken with a camera. I swallowed hard.

"How---"

I didn't finish my sentence.

In order to have gotten these photos, someone had to have gone through a lot of work to find them. I'd thrown all of my past wedding photos away, along with the rings, so whoever sent these photos, had to have gone to people who would have copies.

The families of my deceased spouses.

They're the only ones that would have them. And if the police had shown up on their doorstep, asking for wedding pictures, that could raise a few questions. They could all now be wondering if I'd killed their loved ones, which could mean that Simeon might not be the one behind the madness. It could be anyone, if that was the case.

And looking at the wedding photo of Nino and I, on our wedding day, standing at the altar, meant that whoever had taken it, had been in the audience. They'd been at my damn wedding! Immediately, I regretted deciding not to videotape our wedding day. Nino had wanted to, but I told him that it was a waste of time, and money.

I regretted it now.

"I can explain."

"Explain what? That I'm your 13th husband? Or maybe you want to explain that all of the other ones are dead. Flip the photos over."

I flipped them over. Their death dates, and how they died, were written on the back of each photo.

This wasn't the police's doing. It couldn't be. It was too much information; too much work. This was that stalker's doing, whoever it was. I could feel it.

Not knowing what to say or do, I started to whimper.

"Oh, no, don't cry now. Hell no."

"Nino, it's not what it seems."

He didn't say anything to my comment. He waited for me to pull myself together to speak.

"I didn't tell you, because I mean, telling you that I had twelve dead husbands, isn't exactly pillow talk. But I didn't kill any of them. I may be a liar, but I am not a killer."

"A liar and a killer go hand and hand."

"No. They don't. Not to me. I understand if you don't want to be with me anymore. After all that has happened, and all of the lies, I wouldn't want to be with me either. I know how it all must seem. I didn't tell you, because I didn't want you to be afraid of me. I just wanted to leave it all in the past. But I didn't kill them, any of them, and I haven't been trying to kill you."

Nino walked to the closet and pulled out a bag.

He started to pack some of his clothes, and once he was finished, he looked at me.

"I have no idea who I married. This whole goddamn marriage is a joke!"

"No. It isn't. I love you."

"Says the woman who has been married thirteen times, to 12 other dead men. And not to mention, currently carrying another man's baby! Apparently, you have no idea what love is." Nino stormed out of our bedroom, and after hearing the door slam, Mama Kay appeared in the entrance of the doorway.

"This is one big mess!" I screamed as I went through the wedding photos again, and Mama Kay came to sit next to me.

"We'll fix it," she said.

"How?"

"I haven't figured that part out yet, but we will."

Things between Nino and I were never going to be the same, no matter what she said or did.

She watched me go through the wedding photos.

"Simeon must've sent him those."

"You said that he only had 5 of them though, and if he did send them, why would he send you one too? Your package looked just like this. What was inside of yours?"

Mama shook her head. "Nothing."

"Nothing? Do you mean that it was completely empty? Or nothing like none of my business?"

"I mean nothing Ivy."

"Don't lie to me! Tell me Mama! What was inside of yours?"

"Nothing that you need to worry about. Now, calm down. Let's not forget that you are pregnant. You need to stay relaxed for the baby. You don't worry about anything. I'll fix it. Mama always fixes it," she said, but I knew that there was something that she wasn't saying. There was something that she was hiding. There was something that she wasn't telling me…

And I was going to find out just what it was.

~***~

I'd been driving around for hours, and somehow, I'd ended up somewhere I wasn't supposed to be.

Cage's house.

Nino hadn't been home in over a week, and he'd made it clear that the next step in our story was a divorce.

He'd made it clear that he didn't trust me, or believe a word that I said, and I couldn't blame him.

He almost died, a few times, from what looks to be because of my past, lies and secrets. He deserved better. He deserved someone other than me.

I didn't deserve a happy ending anyway.

In jealousy, I watched Cage's new, beautiful next door neighbor, head up his steps and knock on his front door. The door opened and she went inside.

I changed my mind and my plans, and I started my car.

Even though I was carrying his baby, and even though I'd had plans at that moment to tell him the truth, I decided that it would be best to stick to my words, pretend that the baby wasn't his, and just leave him alone.

I drove away, deep in thought, so much so that the ding noise from my cell phone startled me.

I picked up my phone, with my free hand.

Noticing the e-mail address, I pulled over on the side of the road.

I hadn't received a message from the strange e-mail since the day that I'd deleted my work e-mail from my phone and quit my job.

Ding.

How in the hell did they get my personal e-mail?

And after all of this time, what did they want now?

I opened the e-mail and read the subject.

"All I ever think about is you Malaysia Christina...Deanna Marie...Ivy Raye."

I exhaled.

At the statement, there was no doubt in my mind that this person had sent Nino the pictures to destroy what was left of my marriage.

I briefly wondered if it was Mama's husband Simeon, as she'd suggested.

He could simply be trying to throw me off with his comments, or scare me into admitting something that I didn't do.

Thanks to Mama Kay, if it was him, or the police that he was working with, we were ahead of the game.

I typed: *"All I think about is you too."*

I hit send, knowing that I wouldn't get a reply. They never replied to anything that I said. They would just wait a few days and then say whatever it was that they wanted to say.

Pulling back out into traffic, I continued down the road.

Ding.

The ding surprised me.

"Prove it."

The e-mail said.

"How?" I typed and commented aloud.

Suddenly, I recalled everything that was happening around me.

Nino was leaving me.

Nino had found out the truth about me.

Simeon was trying to get me thrown in jail.

I was pregnant by Cage.

He was dating someone who looked like a model.

Mama Kay was hiding something from me.

Someone was stalking me.

And the same someone knew way too much about me.

JuJu was dead.

And I still couldn't be sure as to who had killed her or who had been trying to kill Nino.

This was just too much.

At that very moment, I thought about running. I thought about heading to the airport, catching a plane, and leaving it all behind. And I wondered if that included Mama Kay.

She knew something that she didn't want me to know, and I wondered if it was something that could change the situation, whether it would make it better or worse.

But her lips were sealed and I didn't like it. Not when my life was hanging in the balance.

Still in my thoughts, I turned onto my street, just in time to see the black car with the tinted windows, pulling out of my driveway.

Nino's truck wasn't there, and without thinking things all through, I pressed on the gas, trying to block them in, but they got past me and hurriedly, drove away. I looked right at the driver's side window, and couldn't see a thing through the tint.

Once they were out of sight, I thought about Mama Kay being inside of the house, and I hopped out of the car and hurried inside to make sure that nothing had happened to her.

"Mama!"

I yelled as soon as I opened the front door, but I found her sitting in the living room, right by the window.

"They were only out there for about five minutes."

I took a seat.

"Did Nino ever teach you how to shoot his gun?" She asked.

"No? Why?"

She stood up.

"I have a feeling that it's time for you to learn."

~***~

I'd been asleep for hours.

I felt the warmth of Nino's body, as he slid in bed behind me. I was surprised that he was there. I had lost count of how many days he'd been gone.

The bathroom door was cracked, with a small piece of light shining out of it.

2:37 a.m. was on the clock and I groaned sleepily, as I prepared to ask questions.

Nino didn't speak as he cuddled up next to me and when I tried to turn over to question him, he whispered "Shhh!" and then flipped me over onto my stomach.

The bed screeched as he made his way behind me.

His touch was warm and gentle.

"Baby, I'm so sorry---,"

"Shhh," he whispered again, and I clamped my mouth shut and obeyed him.

I was naked, as usual, as he continued to caress my back and soon, his touch was replaced with soft and sincere kisses.

I couldn't remember the last time that I'd felt his touch or the last time that I'd been pleased, so despite the fact that we still had 101 unresolved issues, if he was going to give *it* to me…I was going to take it!

He gripped my ass, tightly, and quickly released it with a light smack. I giggled, once he started to lick on my butt cheeks, but honestly, I just wanted the *wood*.

And after showing my body just a little more attention, I was elated once I heard the clinking sound of his belt buckle.

Showtime.

I felt him ease my legs apart, arching the right one, slightly, causing it to bend at the knee. Face down, he took his time, but finally, I felt him slide *it* in.

He paused for only a second as I cooed, and then slowly, he shoved his *pipe*, deeper, and deeper inside of me.

I had a nice grip on my pillow, as Nino started to pound me. The pounds of pleasure started slow and sweet; and then they became rough and dangerous, just like I liked them.

"Ohhh…yes…" My moans grew louder and louder, but the sound of his thighs slapping up against my ass, overshadowed them.

The bed rocked, and I was sure that Mama Kay could hear my screams.

"Oh…Nino…here I---," before I could finish my sentence, I felt his dick plop out of me.

"No! Wait! I was almost there," I whined and I looked behind me.

My heart dropped!

What?

"Ahhhhh! Ahhhhh! Ahhhhh!"

I screamed and kicked as the masked man hurried off of the bed and scrambled out of my bedroom door.

"Ahhh! Ahh!!!"

Seconds later, I heard the sound of the stairs, and I knew that it was Mama Kay running. She ran into the bedroom, flipped on the light switch, and I saw that she was holding a gun.

"Ahhhh!" I screamed again, as I looked at it, and she looked around the room.

"What! What is it! What's wrong!"

She held the gun out in front of her, as I tried to catch my breath.

"Someone…was…here...and they…"

She noticed that I was naked. She disappeared out of the room, without letting me complete my sentence.

I'd thought that it was Nino.

I'd really thought that it was him.

Still trying to pull myself together and once I heard the front door slam, I hurried out of the bed.

Mama Kay appeared and I exhaled.

"What happened?"

"I was asleep. I thought it was Nino, that got into the bed and then we started to…I thought it was Nino, until I turned around, and…it wasn't Nino! It was a man! I don't know who. He was wearing a mask."

I was distraught.

"A mask? Like what kind of mask?"

"A ski-mask."

"Like the one I'd told you that some woman had been wearing that day that you moved in here?"

I nodded. "Yes. But you were wrong. This wasn't a woman. He was all man. Trust me. It was a man," I said to her as she called the police and I called…my husband.

~***~

"So, someone breaks in, you thought that it was me, you have sex with him, but apparently, he wore a condom, and then you turn around, he's wearing a mask, and then he runs away?" Nino asked in disbelief.

"I know it sounds crazy, but it's true."

The night before, I'd called the police and had gone to the hospital.

Though the sex wasn't rape because I'd allowed it to happen, but it damn sure wasn't consensual because they broke in and I'd thought that they were my husband, I'd had a rape kit done.

And the was nothing there.

He'd worn a condom, in the midst of all of that, somehow, I must've missed the fact that he'd put one on, or maybe he'd already been wearing it before he woke me up, but he hadn't left behind any fluids…not even a piece of hair!

"You sure you didn't have sex with him? And pull this stunt, just to get me over here?"

"Nino. Someone was in the house. Now, I don't know what's going on with you two, and it isn't my business," Mama Kay stated, pretending as though she didn't know anything, "But she's telling you the truth. By the time that I'd made it down the stairs, they were half-way up the street," she lied. She'd already told me that she hadn't seen anyone outside that night.

Nino's face softened.

"I thought it was you…"

"So, what do we do?"

"There's nothing we can do."

"No. In general. Let's face it. Someone is doing this, all of this, because of you. Someone who knows the truth about you "Malaysia." Yeah, I figured out a long time ago that that's your real name. The pictures, the hit and run, the poisoning, the e-mails, we all know that this has something to do with you. So, what do we do?"

"We?"

Nino sat down and took a deep breath. "Yes. We. This marriage is shot to hell…you and I both know that. It was built on lies, but at the end of the day, I still care about you. And I don't want anything to happen to you. There's no point in leaving you, to figure this out on your own. Not right now. Not after this. Not like this," Nino pointed at my stomach.

Tears were streaming down my face.

I glanced up at Mama Kay, and she smiled.

"I told you, he was the one."

Yeah. She did.

I nodded at Nino.

Mama Kay spoke again. "I think she needs to learn how to shoot a gun."

Nino nodded.

"And maybe how to put out a fire," she said.

Nino and I both looked at her confused, as she headed for the window.

Nino jumped up, and so did I. Sure enough, the back of his truck was on fire.

"What the f---," Nino went running.

I looked at Mama Kay.

"Did you see anything? Did you see where they ran?"

"Yes."

I looked at her confused. "Why didn't you say anything?"

Nino was outside yelling.

"The masked man was already in the process when he caught my attention, and I didn't stop it because now, there's no way that Nino is going to leave you here alone. And we need him here," she commented, and headed out the front door, to assist Nino.

~***~

I listened to Mama Kay lie to Simeon about why she wasn't coming home. She didn't want him to know that she wasn't coming back for good or that she knew the truth about him.

So, she'd told him all the things that he wanted to hear.

She'd said that she couldn't help but wonder if his obsession over proving that I'd killed his son had turned to something else.

We talked about the e-mails, and that they were always somewhere watching me. We talked about the things that they said. And of course, we couldn't forget about the break-in, and whoever it was that had tricked me into having sex with them. She didn't think that Simeon was capable of all of that, but she couldn't be sure, especially when you started to tie in JuJu's death. Trying to kill Nino, and pin it on me…maybe. But why JuJu?

None of it seemed to fit together, yet in a way, it all seemed connected.

I assured Mama Kay that the man that had been in my bedroom that night wasn't some old fifty-something year old man.

That was someone else. I was sure of it.

The strange e-mails were coming in now, more frequently, since Nino had been staying back at the house. Mostly, they were proof that whoever it was, was keeping a close eye on me, on Nino…on everything.

Watching Nino go outside, once Mama Kay hung up the phone, I spoke to her.

"You know, Simeon isn't really a problem. We both know that he nor the police will find anything. Even if they have their suspicions, we both know that I didn't do anything, at all. So, there's no way that they can pin anything on me, even if they tried. There's nothing there. And if they were trying to kill Nino and put it on me, that didn't work. He's still alive. And now that we know what Simeon has been up to, we've been covering our tracks now, more than ever. All they have is that I've been married thirteen times, and that twelve of my husbands are dead. And that none of them at the time pointed to any foul play on my end. Those are the facts that they have. No matter what Simeon wants them to see. So, maybe you shouldn't waste your energy on him anymore. For your sake. Every time you get off the phone with him, you have that look in your eye."

"What look?"

"Like you are thinking…about protecting me…no matter what that means. No matter who…you get what I'm saying. And I don't want that. No matter what's going on around us. We have enough unwanted attention as it is. You've been here for a while; the room is yours. Besides, I'm going to need you around for your grand baby."

The mention of grand baby made her smile.

Through all of the worrying and stress, I was still pregnant, and I was finally starting to show.

"None of us will be around for the grand baby if we don't figure this out," she said.

"I know, Mama. But there's nothing that we can do about that, now is there?"

"We can leave."

"Now, that sounds like a plan," I said to her.

I'd been thinking about it a lot lately, and I'd already made up in my mind that when no one was expecting it, I was going to disappear.

And I knew that no matter what I said, or felt, Mama Kay was coming with me. She just needed to be honest with me first.

"What are you hiding from me Mama?"

She looked at me confused.

"I know that there's something that you aren't telling me. Tell me."

"I told you, it's nothing."

"I'm sure that it's something."

"I'll tell you when I'm dead," she said and walked away.

"Wait a minute…what!" I screamed after her, but she threw up her hand and just kept walking.

Nino came back inside of the house.

"I've been thinking."

I was unsure of what he was going to say.

"Are you really not going to tell the father about his baby?"

I knew that he wouldn't like my answer, so I didn't say anything.

I thought about Cage, often, especially now that my stomach was getting bigger.

I was thankful that he'd been able to give me something that none of my husbands had ever been able to. But telling him the truth, I felt just wasn't an option for me. Nor did I think it was the best move.

"Aren't you tired of lying, Ivy?"

I felt as though he was judging me.

"I know the truth. Everyone knows the truth…except for him. He deserves to know about his child. What's done is done. Don't keep that from him, especially on the account of me. If for whatever reason I decided to stick around, I would know what I'm getting into. I'm a grown ass man. I can handle it. Just tell that man the truth. You never know what the baby might need. You just never know."

I accidentally smiled.

Though Nino wasn't being all that nice to me, and though I knew that I was probably going to lose him, every day, the fact that he was still there, and the things that he did or said, made me love him more and more.

And I wished to God that there was something that I could do to make him stay.

Well, maybe…there was…

✳✳✳✳✳✳✳✳✳✳✳✳✳✳✳✳✳✳✳✳✳✳✳✳✳✳✳✳✳

Chapter SIX

"Ivy? What's up," Cage greeted me.

The weather was starting to change, and I hid my belly with my charcoal pee coat.

"I just wanted to come by to see how you were doing."

"Really? You drove out of your way, to come see about me? After all of this time?" Cage joked and looked at me with suspicion.

"If you have company, I can come back later," I said, trying to see past him.

"I don't have company. And even if I did…come in," Cage invited me in and slowly, I entered.

I was taking Nino's advice. I decided to tell Cage about the baby. Nino was mentioning how wrong it was to keep the news from the father, every, single day, and then finally, I screamed at him and told him that I was going to tell him.

So, here I was. About to tell him.

It had been some time since we'd had sex, so, I wasn't sure how he would react, but at least he would know. At least I would have done my part.

"Um, forgive me, but I don't know what to say."

"Well, I actually wanted to tell you something," I started.

"Tell me what? That you feel the same way too? That since that day, you haven't been able to get me off of your mind? Is that what you came to say?"

I paused.

"Or what if I said, that if I could turn back the hands of time, I wouldn't have let us miss our chance? I would've taken advantage of all of those moments that we stood out there, talking to each other, laughing and flirting with each other. I would've taken you out on that date, or made a move after our first kiss. I wouldn't..." Cage looked at me. "I wouldn't have let you get away."

Whoa! This wasn't what I'd expected!

Cage walked closer to me. I was still speechless, so I just watched him, watching me, until he was just a lick away from me.

"Tell me that you didn't feel it. Tell me that the connection wasn't there, even before the sex, and that being around me, around each other, doesn't make you weak. Tell me that I'm wrong," Cage whispered. He was so close to my face that I could taste the spearmint gum on his breath.

I started to get hot...real hot, but I kept it all together. There had always been something there, more lust on my end, but it was something. Yet, with everything going on, and with thoughts of Nino popping up in my head, and with the fear that even if in some way we could end up together, knowing that Cage would probably get hurt too, this time, I showed the will power, and I stepped back from him.

"Okay. I guess you don't feel it. My bad."

He started to step away, but I grabbed his hand.

"No. Do you feel it?"

I placed his hand on my hardening belly, and moved it around. Cage looked at me, and then he moved the coat, and exposed my stomach.

"It's yours. My husband knows. Well, he knows that I'm pregnant, but not by you. I lied to him and all he knows is that he can't have kids. It's yours."

Cage's eyes grew bigger than a pair of size B cup titties.

"You're pregnant with my kid?"

I nodded my head yes.

He chuckled for a moment, and then he hit the inside of is right hand, with his left fist. "Hell yeah!" Cage jumped up and down with excitement.

I let out a sigh of relief and a laugh all at the same time.

"You're happy?"

"I've been waiting 37 years to be a father. And you're sure that it's mine?"

I nodded. "Yes. I'm sure."

"And he knows? About the baby? About that day?

"Yes. It was his idea to tell you. Well, not *you* per say; I lied about who the father of the baby was. But he did suggest that I tell whoever the father was, that he was having a child. I just have to find a way to tell him that it's you."

Nino still didn't know that Cage was the father. I knew that I needed to tell him that I'd lied to him in the beginning, but I would cross that bridge when I had to. If I ever had to.

"So, what does this mean?"

"I don't know. I'm still married, to Nino, for now. I'm still trying to figure everything else out," I admitted. In a way, I felt bad, because I didn't want to get Cage's hopes up, thinking that he would get to see the baby and be around.

He wouldn't.

I'd meant what I'd said about leaving as soon as possible, to get away from all of the madness and mess, and I knew that I couldn't take Cage with me.

I could tell that he was still in disbelief.

And then suddenly, it was as though, he'd had a thought. And from the look on his face, not a very good one.

"What? What is it?"

Cage kept his eyes on my stomach.

"Ivy---,"

All of a sudden, nausea punched me in the throat and I started to gag.

"Hold that thought." I remembered where his bathroom was and took off running.

Whosever bright idea it was to call it "morning sickness" must've been high, because I rarely ever got sick during morning hours. It was always in the afternoon, or late at night.

I threw up what was left of my lunch, and headed to the sink. After I washed my hands, I looked for a paper towel. I didn't see any, so I reached for the hanging hand towel, and something on the shelf beside it, caught my eye.

I picked it up.

My heart skipped a beat, and for a moment, I didn't know what to do.

"Oh...My...God!"

I felt so many emotions all at once, that I thought that I was going to explode. I was scared, I was angry, I was confused. Yet, the feeling of being pissed off was what I felt the most, and storming out of the bathroom, I allowed the emotion to have its way with me.

"What the fuck is this?"

I held up the ski-mask.

Cage looked at my hand. "What? No. I can explain..."

"You broke into my house and raped me?"

"What? Rape you? No. Ivy. I didn't. I wouldn't rape you."

"This is the fucking mask! The same mask that someone was wearing, peeping through my windows. The same mask that the pervert was wearing when he came into my house, into my bed, and pretended to be my husband and had sex with me!"

"Ivy, listen, I don't know what you think..."

"I think that you are a goddamn pervert! A stalker and a liar!"

I was livid, and it overpowered my fear, though my head told me that it was probably a good idea to get the hell out of there.

"Was it you? The whole time? Causing all of this hell in my life and in my marriage?"

Cage huffed and walked towards me. "Ivy, No. It's not…" He reached for my arm and I slapped the shit out of him.

"Don't touch me! Don't you ever fucking touch me! And don't even think that you're going to touch my child!" I threw the mask in his face, and I pretty much ran out of the front door. I ran past his new neighbor, girlfriend, or whatever the hell she was, as she was coming up the steps.

"Ivy!"

I heard Cage screaming after me as I got into my car and started to drive away. I looked back in my rearview mirror to see him running out to the street.

I slammed on the brakes.

Cage?

Of all people?

He could've just asked me for some pussy!

Lord knows I would've given it to him!

My mind was all over the place, wondering what else he had been a part of. Wondering if he'd been the one watching me and sending me the e-mails, and maybe even trying to kill Nino. After all of the things he'd confessed to me, only minutes ago, he definitely felt more for me than he'd ever let on.

It could've been him. Doing everything.

The whole time!

And what about that day that Nino was sure that he'd seen someone inside of our house? Cage was close enough to get in, and get out with little to no effort.

Maybe the incidents really hadn't been connected at all. That would make sense as to why certain things were off and never seemed to add up.

Simeon could've been doing things to try to get me to go down for killing my husbands.

And Cage could've been the one stalking me and Nino.

Cage stood in the middle of the street, screaming my name and I made a U-turn. Once he saw me coming back towards him, he started walking towards the car, but once he saw that I wasn't slowing down, he hurriedly, jumped out of the way.

"Ivy!"

I reversed, and pressed on the gas again.

Cage barely got away that time, as he ran, behind his car.

I reversed again, pressed the gas and ran right into it.

"Ivy! Listen!"

The impact was a little harder than I'd thought that it would be and it made me dizzy.

As I reversed, I heard parts of the front of my car fall off and something scraping against ground.

Cage started back at me and I put the car in drive again.

"Okay! Okay! Okay!" Cage said, running in the opposite direction. "Just go! Damn it, Ivy! Just go!" He screamed, making his way to his front porch steps. His neighbor, Sheree, was on her phone, yelling.

I assumed that she was calling the police.

The police.

Trying to run Cage over with my car, wasn't the best look for me, considering Simeon's motives, so, I reversed again, and this time I started down the street, and with a mixture of anger and sadness filling up every inch of my heart, I never looked back.

~***~

Mama Kay had flown to Louisiana to gather her things, and I was in her bedroom, that was in my house.

After discovering the ski-mask in Cage's bathroom, I had been in one hell of a bad mood! I hadn't told Nino, because no matter how I looked at it, I didn't see that situation playing out too good. And I hadn't told Mama Kay because her mind and her actions, couldn't be trusted; especially on a matter such as that.

I was so angry at Cage, but strangely, it wasn't enough to want him to die. I couldn't even say that I wanted to see him in jail, even though what he'd done to me was unnecessary. Not to mention, if he'd been involved of anything else that had been going on.

He just didn't seem like the type to be infatuated or obsessed over anyone, to the point to where he would've done something as crazy as that. He had no need to be. He could have anyone, and I do mean anyone, that his heart desired, even me, so, why break in? Why pretend to be Nino to have sex with me?

The ski-mask was the proof, and even if I wanted to, I couldn't deny it.

Why else would he have it?

And I was having his baby?

I was so disgusted.

Still in my thoughts, I continued to search Mama Kay's room. I pulled out her drawers, and I looked in the closet. I even looked underneath the bed. I knew what I was looking for, and I was going to find it.

Though I didn't want to admit it, mentally, I was breaking down. After all that had gone on, in just a few short months, I was overwhelmed and I just wanted to get away from everything, and everyone.

I heard Nino enter the room behind me.

I knew that he could sense that something was going on with me, but he never asked me what was wrong, or what it was. Still, if I was out of his sight for too long, he would come and find me.

"Ivy?"

I ignored him and continued to look.

"What are you looking for?"

I still didn't answer him.

"Ivy!"

I pushed everything off of the dresser once he shouted my name.

"What!" I screamed at him. "What!"

I slammed my hands down on the dresser and focused on taking deep breaths. I waited to see if he would try to comfort me, but he didn't. Instead, he spoke to me from a distance. "Everything is going to be okay."

"No Nino. It isn't."

Nothing was okay and he knew it.

Our lives had become one big shit show.

I looked at my reflection in the mirror that was attached to the dresser. I could see Nino behind me, with his arms folded across his chest. The image of him, wearing a plaid shirt and khakis, reminded me of Daddy, which reminded me of…

"Nino? Move this dresser out for me."

"Move it out?"

"Out. Up. Whatever you want to call it. Just move it off of the wall."

Nino did as he was told.

I remembered when I was younger, when Mama Kay wanted to hide money from herself so that she wouldn't spend it, or hide something from Daddy so that he wouldn't see it, she would tape it to the back of the mirror attached to the dresser, with duct tape.

Once Nino had the dresser up enough for me to see behind it, I grinned sneakily.

There it was.

The thin package, envelope, that had been delivered to my house for Mama Kay, was tapped to the back of it.

I pulled at the tape until the envelope was free.

"Ivy? Do you really think you should be going through her stuff? Whatever that is, just ask her."

"I did ask her," I commented to him as I opened it.

Nino grew quiet as I pulled the contents out of package. I looked at it.

For a while, I stared at it in confusion.

"What? What is it?"

I stared at it for a little bit longer.

What?

How?

I was puzzled.

I tried to understand what it was that I was seeing, but I couldn't. I didn't understand it at all.

"What is it Ivy?"

I turned what I was holding around to face him.

Nino stared for a while, and then back at me.

"Ivy? Is that…"

~***~

Immediately, I spotted the baby doll, hanging on the front door.

"Wait here," Nino said, and then he pulled out his gun from the glove department. He got out of the car and I watched him.

Things, all sorts of things, had been happening back to back over the last few days.

We'd come home one day to find the house flooded. Someone had come in, stopped up the kitchen sink and both of the tubs in the bathrooms, and left the water running. We'd been gone for almost two hours that day, so imagine the mess that we'd found when we'd returned home.

And then just the day before, after only a ten-minute store run, we'd come back to find hundreds of my wedding photos all over our yard, and I do mean hundreds! They were of each of my marriages, scattered in our yard, on the porch, in the streets and even in the yards of the houses beside us.

It behooved me that all of these things were happening and none of our neighbors ever seemed to hear or see a thing.

And the police were starting to act as though they were getting tired of our phone calls. Maybe it was because they were working to get me, but all they ever did was take a report, and make a few suggestions. They suggested getting an alarm, or moving, but we'd moved already. And they'd followed us. Moving wouldn't help; only disappearing was going to solve this.

And now this.

I watched Nino carry the doll towards the car.

I'd been waiting on him to finally come to his senses and save himself, and leave me there all alone, but he hadn't. At least not yet.

He got into the car.

The baby doll had red paint splatter all over it. One of the eyes were missing and it had a knife stabbed threw a photo that was taped on its chest. The photo was of me.

Recent. Showing my baby bump and everything. The knife had been stabbed right in the center of my belly.

"If you don't go Nino, you're going to die," I said to him.

"What?"

"Just leave me here. If you stay here, you're going to end up dead," I confirmed for him.

"And if I leave you here, alone, so will you."

I looked at him.

"That's the thing. I don't think I will. If they wanted to hurt me, they would've done so already. They went through the trouble of breaking in, pretending to be you, just to have sex with me. They could've killed me then. Whoever it is, doesn't want me dead…they don't want me with you."

I could see his forehead start to wrinkle, which meant that he was thinking.

"Why would they want me dead? What do you know Ivy?"

"I don't know anything. Not for sure anyway. Just go."

Nino took his keys out of the ignition.

"No."

That was all that he said, and the he got out of the car, and waited for me to follow his actions.

I glanced at the doll, and then threw it in the backseat.

Just a few more days.

As soon as Mama Kay was back.

As soon as I heard her explanation for what I found.

As soon if I made up my mind if I wanted to take her with me, or not.

Just a few more days, and I would be free.

I would be gone.

~***~

Mama Kay walked in with her bags, to find me on the couch waiting for her.

"Hey Daughter," she said.

I didn't respond.

Immediately, she dropped her bags and walked over to me.

"What is it Ivy? What's wrong?"

I stared at her.

No matter what she was, no matter what she'd done, I'd always loved her and still did. Most of her sins were on my behalf, but she'd lied to me.

And now, today, she was going to tell me the truth.

"Chile, if you don't open up your mouth and spit it out, I'm going to beat it out of you," she said.

I pulled the package from the side of the couch.

As soon as she saw it, she let out a deep sigh.

I opened the package and pulled out the picture.

"So, I'm confused about something. You see this picture? That's a baby picture of me. And this...this...is you," I said to her as I pointed to the girl that was beside me in the photo.

The photo was of me, and Mama Kay...and then of an older man and an older woman. The strange thing was that the woman in the photo... looked identical to Mama Kay. It was almost like seeing double, like she had a twin.

"Now, at first, I said, maybe these are my grandparents, and you decided to take a small family picture, with all of us in it. But you told me that you'd killed your father when you were just a girl and that I'd never even met my grandmother. So, what I can't seem to understand is..."

"Ivy. I'm not your mother. I'm your sister."

I closed my eyes in shock at the sound of her words. I had them closed for so long that she repeated herself.

"I'm not your Mama Ivy. I'm your older sister," Mama Kay confessed to me, again.

This had been one hell of a week for me!

"When you were born, I was sixteen. On that picture, you were one, and I'd just turned seventeen. I hadn't killed him until a little while after that. I couldn't let him hurt you. I couldn't let him do to you, what he'd been doing to me for all of those years."

Were those tears?

I hadn't seen Mama Kay cry in years, since Daddy's funeral, but there she was, slowly starting to bawl.

"After I made Daddy fall off of the ladder, his death sent Mama into some kind of depression. I didn't understand it. She was free from him, and all of his abuse and torture. I'd saved her. I'd saved all of us. Yet, she missed him. He beat her, cheated on her, raped me, abused me, yet she still missed him."

Nino came through the front door.

When he saw Mama Kay crying, he turned right back around and went back outside. She didn't speak again until we both watched him get into his truck and drive away.

"She stopped talking. Stopped taking care of you. If I hadn't been there, I don't know what would have happened to you. I found her one day. In bed, sedated on pills. She was just lying there, holding his picture, wallowing in her misery. I guess after being controlled, and brainwashed by someone for over twenty years, it could make you feel like you had nothing left. It could make you feel like you couldn't live without them, but for the life of me, I just couldn't understand her. I tried to talk to her. I tried to understand why she wasn't happy about his death, but no matter what I said, she wanted to be with him. So, I gave her, her wish."

My eyes grew wide.

"I didn't kill her. I just told her how to kill herself. I left the choice up to her. I told her exactly how many pills she needed to take in order for her heart to stop beating. In order for her to be with Daddy. I told her if she loved him more than she loved us, she could just kill herself and let us be. But if she loved us, and chose to live, then we could start picking up the pieces of our lives and move on, without him. She had a choice. Love us or leave us behind. And as you can see, she didn't choose me, or you. Until the very end, she chose him."

I swallowed hard, as I digested the truth.

"I went to feed you, and to clean you up and when I came back, she was dead. I was so angry at her. I was older. I could manage. But you. You were so young. You needed her. At that time, I was just about to turn eighteen. No one was going to let me take care of you. Our family wasn't exactly something to be proud of, and I didn't know what would happen to you. So, after I got you down for a nap, I sat there in front of her, for a long while. Her lifeless body sickened me, disappointed me, but I couldn't deny how beautiful she was. Dead and all she was so beautiful…just like me. As you can see, I'm a spitting image of her. Everyone always said so. I looked so much like her that people used to think they were twins; especially once I got older and started to fill out and especially if they'd never seen us before. Maybe that's why Daddy wanted me too. Because I reminded him of her, only a younger, newer version."

I could hear the hate in her voice when she spoke of him. I could see why she'd had no problems with hurting men. I'd known of the awful childhood that she'd had before, but she'd spoken of it with no emotion. Now, whether she wanted to hide her feelings or not, she couldn't.

"When I got the idea, I carried her that day. All the way out to the barn, on the land that her father had left behind. I buried her. Right behind the barn, under the big oak tree. I didn't call anyone or tell anyone, I just buried her and left her there. I placed a rock on top of her grave, so that I would always remember exactly where it was, but I knew as I walked away from her, that I would never come back. I knew that it was goodbye."

She stared off into the distance for a while and then she came and sat beside of me.

"I stared at myself in her mirror for a long while. And then I put on her clothes, pulled my hair back like she used to wear it and put on her lipstick. I put on her earrings and one of her dresses, and for a while, I just stood there. I looked so much like her that it scared the shit out of me. It was like I was looking at her ghost. Then, I heard you cry, and when I walked into your room to see about you, you looked at me, reached for me, and said "Mama". I knew right then that it would work. Taking on Mama's identity would work."

I couldn't believe my ears! I couldn't believe that she wasn't my mother. I couldn't believe that she was my sister. I couldn't believe that all of these years, she'd just been pretending. I just couldn't believe any of it, at all!

"I knew everything about her. Everything. Going from 18 to 32, I knew wouldn't be easy, but I had to try. For you, I had to try. I packed what I could for us in the car that her and Daddy once shared. It was the 80's back then, and so all of our valuables, and all of our money that we had from selling things from our farm, was stashed away in our house. I took it all, everything. All of the money and everything of value, and then I grabbed Mama's purse. All of our important papers, all of hers, everything, and then I wrote a letter. I addressed the letter to the sister right under Mama, Aunt Ruby. She was the second oldest of our 7 aunts and uncles and I told her that I didn't want the farm anymore. I told her that me and my girls wanted to get as far away from that place as possible, and that we never wanted to come back again. I told her that she could have it, and everything in it and just to let us be. They all knew how abusive Daddy was to her…and to me, and I hated them for not helping us. But I can only assume that they understood to get away from the bad memories, because none of them ever came looking."

Mama Kay started to rock back and forth.

"After the letter was in place, I got you settled into the car, and I took off. I had no idea where we were going, and I was thankful that Mama had found the time to teach me how to drive. I just knew that I had to protect you, and keep you safe. And that was all that mattered. All I kept thinking about was if we'd stayed, and you were placed with a family, or someone else, what if your new daddy, was just as bad, or worse than your dead one? I couldn't let that happen. I just couldn't. So, I had to do, what I had to do."

Finally, I was in tears, right along with her. I looked down at the photo again, and then back at her. The resemblance was just down right creepy.

I didn't know what to say.

She'd killed one parent, semi-killed the other, and then she saved me. Took care of me. Loved me and protected me, as though I was her own child, for all of these years.

"I'd officially taken over the identity of Mama; Katie Lyvette. My real name is Daisy June, in case you were wondering. Malaysia is your real name. I picked it out. I'd read it once in a book, and Mama decided to make it your name. She'd initially wanted to call you Faylinda…which is why I told you that you had an Auntie Fay all of those years. Thank God, that she didn't name you that."

I was definitely thankful for that. And she didn't look a thing like someone named Daisy.

"The North was a little better for us, folks of color, at that time than the South, so from Sumter, South Carolina, we made our way to Philadelphia. That's where I met the man that you called Daddy."

Finding out that my real father had been an abusive rapist, versus the one of a kind, charming, smoothest gentleman that I'd ever known, was disappointing.

"We settled right in there. We had a good bit of money, but I sold our car anyway to make sure that we had more than enough. I'd met him on the train. I looked like our mother, dressed like her, and I'd started to talk like her too. No one ever asked questions about me, or my age, or anything, so I'd found a job, and went to work, even when I didn't need to. A nice lady across the hall cared for you, and in return, I not only paid her, but brought her home tons of food from the restaurant that I worked in to help her feed her kids. One night, I got on the train to come home to you, and your "father" approached me. I'd been approached plenty of times, by plenty of men, before him, but I didn't want a man around you. Keeping you safe was my top priority and I knew that if I ever ran across another man like Daddy, I would kill again; I would kill him too. In a heartbeat, for you. But your *father* was different. He made me laugh. He didn't pressure me. He didn't rush me. It took 7 train rides of conversation for me to agree to go on a date with him. And it only took one date for me to know that he was the one, and 5 dates for him to ask me to marry him."

She talked about him, with gratitude…with love.

"And after that, things just got better. They got normal. He took some road work job on the West Coast. He had plenty of family already out there, so it was easy for us to move and adjust. I started college and got into my career. Raised you. Buried him. Continued to do right by you. And now we're here."

She held out her hand, and waited to see if I would grab it. I did.

"After years went by, honestly, I forgot that I was your sister. I truly felt like...*feel* like your mother. Until I saw the picture, reminding me that I wasn't. I didn't know what to tell you, or how to tell you. Or how someone had found it. I left all of that behind. I hadn't taken one single picture with us when I left that day. And to see the photo..." Mama Kay paused. "Someone is digging, and I mean they are really digging around on you and on me. The picture confirms that."

I hadn't even thought about that. It could very well be the police. I'm sure they had the time and resources to trace things back that far, but why would they send her a picture in the mail?

"Everything that I have ever done, good and bad, has always been for you. It might take some time for you to see that..."

I nodded at her.

"I see it. And Okay."

"Just okay? No questions? No fussing at me for keeping the truth from you?"

Everything was over and done with and I felt once again that if she hadn't done the things that she had, the way that she'd done them, I probably would've ended up much worse.

"Yes. Just okay."

She hugged me.

We embraced each other for a long, long time, telling each other how much we loved one another.

Finally, she let me go.

"I guess this means that you can start calling me Daisy now, if you want to," she said.

"No. If it's okay with you, I think I'll keep calling you Mama instead."

~***~

Ding!

Ding!

Ding!

Ding!

The e-mails were coming in back to back.

I could've reported them as spam a long time ago, and though the sender of them was surely responsible for making my life a living hell, I was obsessed with seeing what they had to say.

Nino looked at me and then at my phone.

"Aren't you going to get that?"

Ding!

Ding!

Ding!

"I will in a minute."

I turned my attention back to the T.V.

I hadn't told Nino the truth about Mama Kay. After all, she was pretending to be a dead woman, and not to mention everything else.

I simply told him that Mama had been raped by her father…and that I was the product of that. It explained us both being in the photo, as well as why Mama Kay would've lied to me about being born after they died.

Though he was disgusted by what he thought was the truth, to him, it made sense.

For me, now it made sense as to why Mama Kay looked so young for what I thought was her age. She was almost fifteen years younger than what she was pretending to be.

As far as how we were acting with each other, nothing had change, other than the fact that things felt better between us. I still called her Mama, I still saw her that way, but knowing the truth about her, about me, about everything, made me appreciate her in a whole new way. It made my love for her stronger than ever before. I was grateful that she'd love me enough to do the things that she'd done. I was thankful that she hadn't left back then, without me.

Ding!

Ding!

"Is it the e-mails?"

I nodded. "Yep."

"Mind if I look at them?"

"Nope."

Nino picked up my phone and started to go through the e-mails. The phone continued to ding, even while it was in his hands.

"Don't ignore me."

"You're pissing me off!"

"I miss you."

"I think I'll come and watch you."

Nino read the subject lines one by one.

"And you have no idea who this is?"

I thought about Cage.

It could be him. Thinking of the words that he'd said, before I told him that I was pregnant, and before I saw the mask in his bathroom, it was obvious that he had a thing for me. Something had always been there, but he was never too pressed to show his feelings towards me, but maybe hiding behind the e-mails, was his way of doing so.

Lately, I regretted not hearing him out that day.

What had he wanted to say?

I really wanted to know why he'd done what he did. And I guess a part of me wanted to understand.

"Nope," I answered Nino's question.

If it was Cage, I wasn't sure why I was protecting him. He damn sure didn't deserve it.

Ding.

Nino turned the phone towards me, and then stood up and headed for the door.

"Look Outside."

That's what the subject line said.

Nino walked outside, and came back in, carrying a box. It was long, but I could tell by the way that he was carrying it that it wasn't heavy.

He opened it.

"What is it?"

I could tell that it was a piece of cardboard that had been cut out, but I waited for Nino to turn it around.

The piece of cardboard had been cut into the shape of a tombstone.

Here Lies the Serial Bride.

I scanned the rest of the cardboard.

Malaysia. Deanna. Ivy…

It said and then it listed every, single, last name that I'd ever had, handwritten in permanent maker.

Born: Who Knows.

Death: Soon.

As soon as I'd read the last word, my phone chimed, and I picked it up.

"Have you opened your gift?"

I growled at the e-mail in frustration, and just as I was about to reply, I felt it, for the first time…

A kick.

The baby kicked again, and again, and I couldn't help but to smile. I'd had flutters and something that felt like movement, but these were actual kicks. At that very second, I knew that I couldn't live like this any longer. I knew that I had to protect my baby. At all costs. That was something that I'd learned from Mama Kay.

Mama Kay was all for skipping town, but she'd said that if I was being watched, by the police, or someone other than the police, constantly, leaving wasn't going to be as easy as I'd wanted it to be. And that if we were going to disappear, we had to be smart.

She was right.

And because she was right, and to do what I needed to do as a mother, I knew that meant that I had to find the source of the problem, and deal with it accordingly.

Starting with Cage.

"Ivy? Or should I say Malaysia? I know I've asked you this a thousand times, but are you sure..."

"No. I've never killed one of my husbands."

Nino huffed.

"I could get some cameras put around the house and an alarm system, like the police suggested."

I shrugged.

It didn't really matter what he did.

This wasn't going to stop, unless...

Unless I stopped it.

~***~

"Damn it. I wanted to stop by the store for a ginger ale" I whined to Nino, once we pulled up at home.

"Go ahead in, I'll run to the store right quick and get it," he said.

We'd all just come from my doctor's appointment.

I was having a healthy baby girl!

Mama Kay got out of the car, and after making sure that I had everything, Nino drove away.

I was glad to have a few minutes alone with Mama. There was something that I wanted to discuss with her. There was something that I needed that would require her help.

"Mama, I have a favor to ask you," I started.

The e-mails were still coming. Crazy things were still happening. Nino was run off of the road, just the day before. He'd put cameras all around the house and on the same day, someone had come and destroyed all of them.

I was surprised that he'd left and gone to the store without us, but he knew that Mama Kay had a gun and that she would protect me, if she had to.

"What is it Daughter?" She asked.

"I know that I said that I would never ask you again, but…"

"Nino?"

"No. Cage. I think…"

"Katie!"

We both turned around at the top of the porch steps.

It was Simeon.

Mama Kay's husband and my dead sixth husband's father.

"What are you doing here Simeon?" She asked him.

He seemed to be drunk. Or maybe he was just upset.

"So, you're leaving me?"

Mama Kay told me that he was away on a business trip when she'd gone to get her things.

"Yes. I am. Why are you here?"

Simeon grumbled.

"Why are you here? And why are you leaving me?"

"Do I really need to give you an explanation?" she asked.

"It's because of her. It's always because of her."

Simeon looked at me.

He noticed my stomach and appeared to be surprised.

"She's pregnant. The killer bitch is finally pregnant!"

Simeon screamed.

Mama Kay growled, and stepped forward, but I grabbed her arm.

"Oh no, no, no, no! You don't get to have a baby! Not after all you've done!"

At the conclusion of his words, I knew that things were about to take a turn for the worse.

Simeon pulled out a gun, and both Mama and I gasped.

"You took my son away from me. And how many other sons did you take away from their families? Huh?"

I didn't answer him.

Mama Kay talked to him, but he ignored her.

My heart was racing. I was scared.

"I asked you a question bitch!" Simeon waved the gun and screamed at me.

"None!"

He shook his head.

"Liar! You killed my boy! You killed them all! You had someone to do it for you! Didn't you? And we are going to catch you too! We're so close!"

His statement confirmed Mama Kay's findings and suspicions. It confirmed that he'd been working with the police.

"Simeon, just leave. Go on."

"Oh. I'm not going anywhere. Not until I get what I came here for. Do you know how hard it was, to pretend to love you?"

I looked at Mama Kay's face, right after his statement. It was blank.

But on Simeon's face, I could see that he was a man with nothing to lose.

"I knew from the start that my son hadn't died by coincidence. Wrong place, wrong time, my ass! Oh no, I knew that it was you. When I watched your face at his funeral and your fake mourning, I knew that you knew the truth about what had happened to him. No one wanted to listen to me. Everybody wants proof. I gave up my life, just to follow you all over the goddamn place! State to state, husband to husband, finding proof! I took what I had to three different police stations, until one finally believed me. I showed them everything that I'd had on you. Everything that I'd found. Still, it wasn't enough. Not enough to nail you. They believed me, but they needed more. So, I turned my attention to you," Simeon looked at Mama Kay. I looked at her too.

She seemed unbothered, but she had to be shitting bricks, just like I was.

"I followed you around. Something told me, if I could just get close enough to you, maybe you could give me something that I could use against her. I was right behind you guys one day, as you walked through a mall. You told her about the cruise. She said that she couldn't go, and you told her that you would go alone. Hell, I needed a little vacation myself. It was perfect. Luckily, there was still room on the cruise for me. I looked all over for you, for two whole days. And then finally, I saw you sitting there."

Simeon was still waving the gun, and I wondered if Mama Kay's was in her purse.

"You were lonely. Didn't take much work, especially once sex was involved. You'd spent your life chasing her around, that you'd neglected yourself and what you needed. You were all caught up, once I started giving you this *wood*. I knew that I had you then," he said.

"First of all, your dick is little Simeon," Mama Kay confessed, and I had to force myself not to laugh. "I've never been satisfied from it. Your mouth, yes. But your Jimmy is a junior, sweetie. Never quite hit the spot, if you know what I mean."

Simeon laughed aloud, crazily. "You and I both know that isn't true. You were in love with all this," he said grabbing his junk as though he was a teenage boy.

"You thought that I was in love. I've never loved anybody, but her," Mama Kay said to him, and his facial expression became angry.

"See, that's the problem, right there! I knew about the name changes, the different husbands, but when I would ask you about her," Simeon pointed the gun back at me,

"You would lie. You would lie about her name, where she was, who she was with. You would protect her. So, I knew that there was something there. I knew that you were lying about her for a reason. I thought marrying you would make you trust me more. I thought your loyalty would shift to me, but it never did. I allowed you to run back and forward, hoping that eventually, you would lead me to the *well*, but you never did. Her husbands were still dying, while she was still alive."

In the distance, I spotted my car, which Nino was driving, turning onto our street. I let out a sigh of relief. I looked around at the other six houses of our little cul-de-sac. I wondered why no one had heard the yelling lunatic or looked out of their window to see a crazy man waving a gun. Then again, it was the middle of the day. Kids were at school, and normal people were at work.

But Nino was coming to the rescue.

Suddenly, Nino stopped the car, a few houses up, from our house. Mama Kay was busy shouting at Simeon. I was sure that she was doing it to keep his attention.

Simeon was shouting back at her, still waving the gun, as Nino opened the car door.

"13 husbands. 12 dead. This madness has got to stop!"

I was listening to Simeon, every few words, but my focus was on Nino.

Mama Kay was keeping Simeon talking as Nino made his way down the street, slowly sneaking up on Simeon from behind.

"Evidence. We need more evidence! What more do you need? Twelve dead bodies aren't enough? The name changes, moving state to state, the types of "accidental" deaths...none of that is enough?" Simeon kept the gun in my direction.

"I'm right about you. And if no one else will help me get justice, well, I'm just going to have to take it, myself."

Simeon walked just a little bit closer, not knowing that Nino was about to pounce on him.

And then suddenly...

Nino's cell phone started to ring, and Simeon looked back at him. Nino dived forward, but quickly, Simeon turned back around, and I knew that he was going to pull the trigger.

And he did.

Simeon fired the gun.

"No!!!"

I heard Mama Kay's voice before I'd noticed that she'd leaped in front of me.

It was like déjà vu as the bullet struck her in the chest, and she fell backwards onto me.

It was like watching JuJu all over again, except this time, the woman in my arms, was the love of my life.

I watched Nino tackle Simeon, as I slowly, made my way down to the porch with Mama.

"Mama? Mama? It's going to be okay. Everything is going to be okay," I cried as I tried to assure her. I was shaking uncontrollably. She just looked at me, as I held her in my arms.

"Call 911! Nino! Please! Call 911!"

I could see Simeon lying on his back, as Nino now held the gun on him. Simeon had his hands on his head, as though he was disappointed, that he'd shot her, instead of me.

"Mama, stay with me."

Mama Kay touched my stomach. And then she touched my hand.

"When you were little, I would watch you sleep in your crib," she whispered. "I would sit there for hours. I told you that I would always be there. I told you that I would always help you. I promised to protect you." Mama Kay coughed and I howled at the sight of the blood, oozing out of the sides of her mouth.

"And I did it. I kept my promise to you. I did it."

I was crying hysterically as I rocked her.

"Yes. You did. I was so lucky to have you. And I can't lose you. Please don't leave me. Please."

I cried so hard, that I could barely see her through my tears.

"Please don't go. Please don't leave me Mama."

I felt Mama Kay slowly raising her hand, to touch my face.

"Please. Help is coming. Please don't go."

Somehow, through the pain, she found a way to smile.

"I…am…my…sister's keeper," she pushed the words out of her mouth, just before she closed her eyes. And took her very last breath.

"Oh God, no! No!"

Nino looked at me, just as the sound of the ambulances wailed in the distance. When they finally arrived, they literally had to pry her out of my arms. Nino ran to me, as Simeon was placed into a police car in handcuffs.

He held me as I broke down, from watching them place Mama Kay into a black bag and as I watched her lifeless body disappeared behind the zipper.

My mournful cries caused every single person to stand still for a moment, just to sympathize and listen.

No one, for all of ten seconds, moved. They just stood there, watching me, and some of them looked as though they wanted to cry too.

Finally, they loaded her up, and the police tried to collect information from me, but I started to run behind the van that was pulling off with Mama inside of it.

"No! Bring her back! Please! I need her! Bring her back!"

What was I going to do without her?

Nino chased me and screamed. He caught up to me and wrapped his arms around my stomach. The van carrying Mama, disappeared, and I started to punch at Nino, for getting in my way. He just stood there, and allowed me to hit him. He continued to hold me, and he wouldn't let go.

Finally, I grew tired, and I knew from the spinning of my head, that I was about to faint. But just before I closed my eyes, one last thought crossed my mind.

My Mama, my sister, my best-friend, gave her life, just to save mine. And I would be damned if I was going to let anyone else take that away from me!

No matter what, through all of this, I had to live.

~***~

"Please Ivy, just listen."

Cage had shown up at the funeral home.

He'd had to have been following me.

He had to know that I was alone.

Nino had been on me like bees harassing a comb full of honey, but I'd asked Nino if I could go to the funeral home, to decide on Mama Kay's arrangements, alone.

He didn't like it, but he hadn't had a choice but to respect my wishes.

The arrangements hadn't taken long at all, primarily, because I'd just requested them to cremate her. I'd purchased a beautiful urn, brought it to them, and told them that I would be back to get her.

A funeral or ceremony wasn't necessary. We didn't have family, all there had ever been was us.

And now, there was just me.

"As you can see, or as I'm sure you know, my mother is dead. I don't have time for this today. So, if you would leave me the hell alone, that would be great," I said and tried to rush past him.

"No. Don't go out. There's something that I need to tell you."

Cage looked back and forth from me, down to my belly. After what he'd done to me, and with what I was feeling, I didn't want to hear anything that he had to say.

I ignored his plea and started to push at the door.

"You're in danger, Ivy," Cage blurted out.

I froze.

"Listen to me. You are in danger. Let me help you."

I took a deep breath before turning around.

"You need to get as far away from Nino as possible."

Nino?

Why was he bringing up Nino?

"There's a lot about him…about me…that you don't know. But this is about you, and my child..."

"*My* child!" I roared at him.

A few people walked past us, and Cage waited until we were alone again.

"Look. Nino isn't who you think he is. He's a lunatic! He's obsessed. And he works…for me."

What?

"Well, for the police…well, kind of."

I looked at him confused.

"We've been following you, your case, for over two years, since you moved to Virginia. Yes. Simeon was working with us too. He's the one that brought you to us. We nick-named you "The Serial Bride".

Once he said the words, instantly, I thought of the cardboard tombstone. I remembered the death threat written on it, and immediately I knew that there was probably some truth behind his words and that he couldn't be trusted.

"He had all of the stories, the pictures of you with different husbands, in different wedding gowns, that he'd gotten from the families of the deceased. I was the detective brought in on the case. It was my call. After looking at the accidental deaths, the deaths that occurred by coincidence, and the money that you'd received from a few of them; and not to mention the state hopping and name changes, I thought that this was going to be the case of my career. There was enough there to at least pursue it; JuJu agreed."

JuJu?

Wait a minute…what did he just say?

"Did you just say JuJu?"

"JuJu was my partner on this. Simeon was sure that this was something that you enjoyed, and he knew that soon you would have your next husband, and not long after that, your next victim. So, we acted quickly. JuJu was placed at the job to get close to you. Keep an eye on you at work, to become your friend. If you remember, she started there the exact same day as you. And I…"

Cage paused.

"I was supposed to become your next husband."

I shook my head.

Cage, JuJu, Simeon, and Nino, all…working together? All to get me?

"I was supposed to "wow" you, and get you to marry me, and then see what happened next. See if you tried to kill me or have me killed and only this time, you wouldn't succeed because we all would've been prepared. Catching a Serial Killer Wife was huge! A huge story for our department, and for all of our careers. We knew that you had to have help, or to be paying someone to do the dirty work for you, and we knew if we got you, we got them, we solved the case."

His words made me think about the fact that Mama Kay had died with her secret. I would never know who had been helping her out all of these years.

"But I couldn't do it. The more, and more that I got to know you. The more that I talked to you. The more that I flirted with you. When I started touching you and kissing you, I started to develop real feelings for you and…I just couldn't do it. So, then there was Nino. He used to be an officer, who is now more of a Psychologist. He's the one that evaluates the serial killers, before prison trails and sentencing, to see why they did the things that they did. To pull every ounce of truth from their bodies, and get them the punishment that they deserved. He wanted the job. He was perfect for it. His ability to *not* get attached, was what we needed. It wasn't something that we normally did, but with his skills, and expertise, there was no doubt that he couldn't deliver. And what he was being paid upfront, on top of what he would be paid if he cracked you and took you down, he was all in. Consumed with doing his job, and doing it well."

I felt so betrayed, that I couldn't put it into words.

And I was so angry that I was sure that steam was coming out of both of my ears. All of them had played me like a fool!

"He started on you. I watched him and you, somewhat in jealousy, but more so out of concern or maybe it was the crazy want to protect you. From him. From us. From the case. Somewhere along the way, I think I fell in love with you, and so did JuJu. In a strange way, we thought that just maybe you really were innocent, and that all of it, all of the deaths really were accidents or coincidences. We wanted to save you. We tried to talk Nino off of the case; well not exactly. We would make suggestions at the meetings, and JuJu and I would never have anything that could be used. But Nino was all in and he was sure that something was there. He was sure that you were guilty. So, JuJu and I started to plan against him."

My stomach was in knots, and it started to cramp. Cage reached out to help me take a seat, but I moved away from him.

"I'm the one who ran over Nino."

I looked at him, eyes wide, mouth open.

"Clarke and JuJu baited him to the café. Clarke works with us too. Clarke and JuJu were a thing. And they had been for years. The case made it where they couldn't be together for a while like they wanted to. But he loved her so much, and though he didn't agree with our plan, he would've done anything JuJu asked him to."

What!

Clarke was in on it too? And he and JuJu were a lot more than they'd pretended to be. That's why he was outside of her house, and everything that JuJu had said about the man that she loved being in love with me, must've been a lie. She must've been to see if she could get some kind of truth out of me.

"Clarke called Nino, and told him that he wanted to talk about some things concerning you. JuJu showed up with him. They stood out there and talked for a while, and when Nino headed for his car, I drove by, in an unmarked car and I hit him. It was supposed to kill him, but it didn't. Clarke left the scene and then JuJu called you."

This was crazy! The past two and a half years of my life had been a part of one big lie! One big scheme to take me down for something, that I really didn't do.

"Killing him was the only way. The only way to get him off of the case. JuJu and I had come to love and adore you, and we knew that he wasn't going to stop, until he got the truth out of you. We'd thought about the fact that if he died, it would make you look suspicious, but it still wouldn't be enough to put anything on you. I would verify that I was watching you at your house the whole time, and the case would still be at a standstill. It would've still looked like a coincidence. And eventually, with neither of us bringing anything to the table, the case would've been closed. We'd tried. But Nino lived. And that made things even worse. He was so angry…at you. Angry because he thought that it was you who had really tried to kill him. And that just added fuel to an already raging flame."

"So, all of this time, it has been you trying to kill him?"

"No. That was the only time. The poisoning, putting gasoline in his truck, and all of the other crazy things that he reported, that wasn't us. We started to think that it really was you."

I shook my head.

"No. It wasn't me."

Cage looked confused.

"And JuJu? Who shot her?"

Cage shook his head. "We don't know. To this very day, we have been looking for her killer, but we don't have any leads. We don't know who killed her or why she was killed."

I was silent, so he continued to speak.

"The random things that's been happening to you; the suspicious acts at your house, the harassment, the things still happening to Nino, the e-mails, those aren't us Ivy. Nor did I, or any of us break into your house and assault you. I would never do that to you."

"But I saw the mask."

"The mask that you saw was Sheree's. She replaced JuJu. She's a part of our team. If you don't believe me, the black car, with the tinted windows, is a few cars down from yours outside. She's inside of it. I'm supposed to be in here, spying on you. Sure, we have been having a little fun with each other, but she doesn't know how JuJu and I felt about you, so she was doing her own catching up. She'd followed you around a little bit, made a few runs to chat with Simeon and she'd said that she'd been caught peeping into the window of your new house, but that she'd had on the mask, so no one saw her face."

Mama Kay had said that it was a woman. She was right after all.

"She came straight over to my place that night. She forgot the mask. I placed in the bathroom. She always forgot to take it with her. But the night that someone broke into your house, wearing a similar mask and assaulted you, it wasn't me Ivy. And it wasn't Nino or Simeon. They both were accounted for. The person that broke in, and…had sex with you, was someone else. No one on our team Ivy. No one working the case."

I placed my hands on my head. It was so much information, to take in, all at once, and my head was starting to hurt.

"You have to get away from Nino."

"Why?"

"Why? Have you not been listening to me? I'm trying to save you."

His comments reminded me of Mama Kay.

"He's obsessed Ivy. Obsessed with you and this role. Playing mind games is what he does best. You can't believe anything that he says. For instance, of course, he isn't a CPA, not at all, so when you offered him the $50,000 to start a business, why do you think he never started it? And that day, meeting the Realtor at some building, he told us that when he got inside, someone really had put an offer in on the building, and the Realtor only met him, to see if he would place one higher. Of course, he was only seeing it for show, so he didn't, and they spent the majority of their time inside of it, talking about sports. But he told us that he used the opportunity, to try to pull some things out of you. He told you that the Realtor gave him a message. That was all his doing. All his idea and his words. His way of throwing out things, piece by piece, in hopes of getting your confession."

Nino had to have told him about the conversation that day. Otherwise, how else would he have known?

"Most of the time that he was bringing you information, or saying that someone told him something, majority of the time, it was a lie. He already knew it. He was just trying to get you to tell him more. And after you got pregnant, even though he knew it wasn't his, why do you think that he stayed?

"Because he loves me."

"No. Because he has a purpose. Because he had a role. Because he had a job to do. He didn't care about any of that, or who else you were sleeping with, other than him, all he cares about is getting the "win". I knew that you were pregnant, before you told me, but Nino reported that you'd been sleeping with someone at your job. I didn't know if there was a possibility of it being mine, especially after hearing that, so when you told me, that it was my baby, I really was surprised."

"I'd lied to him. I didn't want him to know that it was you. I never slept with anyone from work. I lied."

Cage didn't comment on what I'd said.

"Nino isn't like most people. He doesn't feel like most people do, which is why we'd hired him in the first place. We knew that his feelings wouldn't get in the way of doing his job. His heart is as cold as all of the psychopaths that he's interviewed over the years. He doesn't care about you Ivy. All he cares about is solving this case. And he won't stop, until he does."

If what Cage was saying about Nino was true, he'd played it all so well. I didn't see any of it. I didn't see what Cage was trying to make me see.

"So, the e-mails aren't staged from you? Then who's sending them?"

Cage shrugged. "Unless Nino is doing it on his own, somehow, and not reporting it, we don't know who is behind that either."

"What about the pictures? The ones sent to Nino? And the one sent to Mama?"

"What pictures?"

"Of me and all of my husbands."

"He has access to those."

"No, they were in the same package, addressed to him, from the same handwriting as Mama Kay's."

"We never sent pictures to Nino, or anything to your mother. That wasn't us Ivy."

"What about the cardboard tombstone?"

"No. Ivy. Not us."

"And you admit that you were the one responsible for the hit and run, but that's it?"

"That's it. That was for you."

Then what am I missing?

"It could've all been Nino; except for the poisoning thing, because he was just as upset about that as he was about the hit and run. He was sure that you were trying to kill him. And to this day, he is still sure of it. He thinks that you are trying to play the victim role, and making up stuff, because you are planning something. He thinks that you are planning his murder and your escape. But if you are saying that truly it wasn't you poisoning him, and all of the other mishaps, then, Ivy, I don't know what to tell you. I guess the law isn't the only ones who have it out to get you."

I stood up.

"After Simeon's scene, and after killing your mother, the head, my boss's boss, came down and called the whole operation off. We are supposed to immediately, stop pursuing the case, and stop pursuing you. But Nino disagreed. He told me himself that he wasn't going to stop; not until he accomplished what he'd signed up to do. He said that they would thank him in the end. So, he plans to continue. He's very unstable Ivy. This whole thing has brought out the monster in him. You're in danger. I can't be sure what he will do to you, or to the baby, just to get the truth. I don't trust him, and if he hurts you…or my child," Cage bit his lip.

I was relieved that I'd been wrong about him; well, I wasn't happy about the truth or about lies either, but at least he hadn't been the masked man who had taken advantage of me.

But then, who was?

"Leave Ivy. Change your name again, and do whatever you do, however you do it, just leave. If you don't want me to be a part…of this, I understand, but do me a favor, and just go."

Cage begged me and I could see the sincerity in his eyes, but I wasn't going anywhere.

Not yet. Not still knowing that someone else, was still out there watching me. At this point, and if he was telling the truth about everything else, Cage was the only protection that I had.

I could tell that as long as I was there and carrying his child, and still around Nino, then he wouldn't be too far away. He would be looking out for me. And he wouldn't let anything happen to me.

So, for the time being, I was going to have to stay.

I wobbled towards the door, with Cage waiting to hear a word from me.

"This is a lot to take in. Right now, I'm only concerned about my baby…our baby. So, until I can figure things out, I'm expecting you to protect me. To protect us, no matter what," I played on his emotions.

Cage nodded his head.

"And by the way, you, all of you were barking up the wrong tree. This whole time, my *sister* was killing my husbands…not me."

****

Chapter SEVEN

"Are you hungry?" Nino asked.

I was, but I shook my head no.

I wasn't eating anything that he was offering me.

Since the talk with Cage the other day, I'd been paying attention to every little thing that Nino said and did.

If Cage was telling the truth, Nino sure as hell was good at his job, because since I'd been watching him, I hadn't noticed anything that I would consider suspicious or that I could call a red flag.

"I like the urn that you picked out for her. It's nice. I still can't believe that she's gone," Nino said, sitting the food in front of me, anyway.

Instantly, my stomach started to growl.

"So, what now?"

I asked him, fighting to resist the plate of hot wings.

"About what?"

"Us? Everything?"

Nino sat down next to me.

"I've been thinking about that. With your Mama gone, you don't have anyone else."

"I can manage," I said to him.

"I'm sure you could, but I was thinking maybe we could try to manage together."

I stared at him.

"After everything, you still want to stay around?"

Nino shrugged and took a bite of his chicken.

"I ain't got nothing else to do," he chuckled.

Cage said that he wouldn't want to go anywhere. That he planned to stick around until I gave him what he wanted, what he thought was truth.

"So, do you think that Simeon was the one trying to kill me? And causing all of this mess?" Nino asked.

"I don't know."

Cage admitted to running over Nino, but he promised that he'd had nothing to do with everything else.

Simeon could've been the one behind some of the other things, but since I was still receiving e-mails, I was willing to bet that he wasn't.

"I was sure that it was you. No offense. I mean, with your other dead husbands and all, all arrows pointed to you." Nino paused, and then he said, "Come on, if it was you, you can tell me," he made a joke out of it, but I knew that he was serious.

Nino was trying to take me down for murders, that I didn't commit. I might have stood by and let them happen, or made a request or two, but I didn't do it.

"What if I told you that I did it, then what? I didn't kill anyone, but what if I had killed them Nino? Then what would you do? Would you stay? Or would you turn me in to the police?"

Nino sucked a chicken bone.

"Depends on the reward," he laughed, but I didn't.

I knew right then, that Cage had been telling me the truth.

Now what?

"Well," I said to Nino, taking one of his chicken wings, instead of eating the ones that he'd placed in front of me. "Lucky for you, I'm not a killer."

"Why am I the lucky one?"

"Because if I was some "serial bride", you would be dead already. After all, aren't they?"

I could tell by the tensed look on his face, that the wheels were turning inside of his head.

~***~

Nino was watching my every move.

Everywhere I went, he wanted to go. If I was in one room, he was in there too. I had been trying to find a way to get away from him, so that I could talk to Cage, but he was making it pretty much impossible, while still keeping up the concerned husband image, who just wanted to protect me.

Maybe it was because they'd officially closed the case, and now he felt as though he was in a rush to find out the *truth*, and maybe he thought that being around me, constantly, that I was bound to make a mistake.

But I was on to him, and for the most part, I just wanted him to let me breathe.

"Nino, I don't feel good," I lied to him.

He walked over to me, and observed me.

"What's wrong? What do you need me to do?"

"I don't know. I think I'm getting a cold. My throat is sore."

"Well, you're pregnant, so there's not much that you can take. You have some ginger ale in the refrigerator."

"What about soup?"

I knew that we didn't have any, I'd already checked.

Nino disappeared for a while, and then he came back into the room.

"We don't have any. I'll run to the grocery store and get some. What kind?"

"Chicken noddle," I confirmed for him, and he nodded, grabbed his coat, and I listened for him to pull out of the driveway.

I got out of the bed, slipped on the only pair of jeans that I could fit, grabbed my coat and headed to the living room. I picked up my purse, and reached for my keys, only to find that they weren't hanging on the key rack where I'd put them.

Where are my keys?

I looked through my purse.

They weren't there either.

After searching for a long while, and not finding them, I got the feeling that I was searching for nothing.

Did Nino take my keys?

Who in the hell does he think he is?

I grabbed my phone.

I groaned realizing that since I'd gotten a new phone that I didn't have Cage's number. I also noticed a few of the e-mails, but opening them was the last thing on my mind.

Nino was really bugging!

He hadn't taken my purse, so I could just call a cab.

Yeah. That's what I was going do. I found the number to a cab, but just as I was about to call the number, I heard Nino's truck pulling back into the driveway.

Hurrying to my bedroom, I undressed and climbed back into bed.

Shortly after, I heard Nino's footsteps coming down the hallway.

"I'm back. I'm about to make your soup."

I groaned, and once he disappeared, I waited a while before getting up, and heading to the kitchen.

"You could've stayed in bed. I was going to bring it to you."

I ignored his comments, and glanced at the key rack.

My keys were back.

They were hanging there, on the hook where I'd left them the first time. He'd put them back up there.

"What were you doing up?"

I looked at him.

"When I left. You got up. You moved your purse," he said. I looked at the purse on the counter.

"Oh. I remembered that I hadn't taken my prenatal vitamins today. I had to come and get them out of my purse."

I saw Nino glance at my purse to see the bottle.

"Oh."

He continued making the soup, and I watched him, feeling something like fear.

Right then, and there, I wished that I'd taken Cage's advice.

I should've packed a bag, and caught a flight.

~***~

"Excuse me, Mrs. Parker?"

"You heard me. I need to go. Now!"

I was at my doctor's appointment.

Nino was waiting for me back in the room, while I was supposed to be going to pee in a cup.

The nurse looked at me confused.

"If he asks, tell him that I'm still in the bathroom," I said, reaching her the cup, and heading for the door.

This was my only chance to get away from him, and I was taking it! I'd carried my small arm pouch on purpose that day, so he wouldn't ask why I was taking my purse with it, and with it on my wrist, I removed my phone from it and called a cab.

I headed out of the door, and wobbled as fast as I could. The cab said that it would take fifteen minutes, but I knew that I didn't have that kind of time.

Nino hadn't let me breathe, move, sleep, or even eat without being all over me in the past few weeks, and I was sick of it. I couldn't take it anymore. And I knew that it wouldn't be long before he came looking for me.

I spotted the city bus.

"Wait! Wait!"

They held the door open for me.

"How much is it?" I held out a twenty.

Though we all knew that it was too much, the woman took it from my hands, and nodded for me to take a seat.

The bus slowly stared to pull off and I stared at the doctor's office, wondering when I would see Nino come running out the door, but I didn't.

As the building disappeared, I took a deep breath.

I'd made sure to put everything that was important to me in my small pouch. I never had to go back to that house. The only thing that I was refusing to leave behind was Mama Kay's ashes, and I was headed to Cage to see if he would get them for me.

Then, I was getting on a plane, and never looking back.

It took over an hour for me to finally arrive at the bus stop that would lead me to Cage's house. Before getting off of the bus, I checked to see if his car was there…it was. I also looked to see if the black car that his "partner", Sheree, drove was in the driveway; it wasn't.

I hurried off of the bus and knocked on his front door.

Cage cracked the door, and once he saw that it was me, worry quickly spread across his face, and he made space for me to come inside.

"You were right," I said immediately, walking into his house. I was cold, and thirsty.

"What did he do to you?"

I headed to his sink, grabbed a cup and turned on the water.

"Nothing. It was like he was keeping me hostage. He wouldn't let me breathe. Everywhere I went, he went. If I would fall asleep, I would wake up to him just sitting there, watching me. And one day, he even stole my keys."

Cage looked angry, mixed with concern.

"He's obsessed over this, over you. And the truth."

"His truth. I told you. My sister killed my husbands."

"You don't have a sister."

"Trust me, I do."

Well, I did, I thought to myself.

Cage didn't reply.

"I just need for you to go over there, to my house, and get Mama Kay's urn with her ashes in it for me. And then I'm going to take your advice and disappear."

Cage watched at my stomach.

"When are you due?"

"I still have a little while to go. I'll be settled by then."

"Is it a…"

"It's a girl."

"Where will you go?"

Even if I knew, I wouldn't tell him.

"If you're wondering if you'll ever see me…or the baby again, once I'm gone. You won't."

He wasn't pleased with my comment.

"But what if I want to?"

"It just wouldn't work, Cage. All I need is for you to get Mama Kay's ashes for me. Can you do that? Can you get them so that I can do what I need to do to keep your daughter safe?"

"Nino isn't going to hand the urn over, Ivy. Furthermore, he knows that I wouldn't be caught near that house…knowing that we were undercover. He would know that something is up. You're going to have to leave without them."

I shook my head.

"I'm not leaving without Mama."

Cage fussed a little while longer, and knowing that I'd meant what I said, he said that he would try.

He assured me that Nino would be looking for me.

"Where's your phone?"

"It's going dead."

"Turn it off and don't turn it back on, for anything. If he can't reach you, he'll get someone to trace it. You can stay here, until we figure this out. Don't open the door, for anybody. Don't worry, Sheree doesn't have a key, and I'll keep her close to me, and away from here. If...and only if, you need it, if something happens, there is a gun in my top left drawer."

I nodded.

"Keep the blinds shut. I'll be back. Help yourself to anything."

And with that, Cage was gone.

I pulled out my phone.

Nino had called me over fifty times.

There were also ten e-mails, just waiting for me to read them, but I didn't. Instead, I turned my phone off like Cage told me to, and though I wasn't in danger, I headed to get his spare gun.

Hours went by, and it started to get dark. I heard Cage pull in, and I saw Sheree pull in next door right after him. Secretly, I watched them.

She was coming on to him, but clearly, he was blowing her off. After some time, finally, she released him, and he headed inside.

He flipped on the light to find that I'd been standing there in the dark.

He didn't have the urn in his hands, and I was disappointed.

"He's looking for you," Cage said.

"Did you go to the house?"

"No. He's there waiting for you, to see if you would come home. He called in, asking for a trace on your phone. He was told that the case was over, and that they wouldn't do it. From what I heard, he wasn't happy about it. But he has a few of his own connections. So, more than likely, he got it done."

Cage took off his coat.

He noticed the gun on the coffee table, but he didn't say anything.

"He'll be tracing your phone. Probably tracing your credit cards too. There's unlimited possibilities in the world of the law, and plenty of favors being done daily. The good thing is that he doesn't know anything about us, or that you're carrying my child, so it won't cross his mind that you could be here. I'll get you a car. You can hit the road tomorrow. I'll give you some cash, and then once you're far enough away, go inside of the bank to get your own money, don't use your cards. Not for a while. Maybe even change your name, again."

I heard him, but I had to take her with me. "I can't leave without her, Cage. After all, I mean, if he finds me, it's not like he can make me go with him, or make me do anything that I don't want to do."

"True. But even you said that his behavior is scaring you. That's why you ran. That's why you're here. You can't trust him, especially now that he knows that he's freaking you out enough for you to take off like that. The only two options you have is to go…or stay, until I can get you what you want."

"You sure your little girl-friend won't mind?"

"She's not my girl-friend, and hiding you, means not even she will know. But you have to promise me, as soon as I find a way to get the ashes, that you will leave."

"I promise."

We talked for a while, and then he told me that he was going to run me a bath. Once I was comfortable inside of the tub, he asked me if it was okay to come in.

He sat on the toilet.

"Has anything else strange happened, since Mama Kay's death?"

"The e-mails still come. They aren't coming from Simeon, right?"

"Nah, he's still in jail. That's another thing, I'm sure they'll be looking for you, regarding that too. To testify, and I'm sure your husbands' deaths will come up...all of them."

I hoped that Simeon died a slow, agonizing death, for killing my Mama. He'd had no right to take her from me.

"Yeah. As I said, I still get e-mails. I was barely checking them these days. If they were going to do something, to me, they would've done it by now. I feel like it's someone messing with me, or out to give me a hard time."

"But who? Why?"

"I don't know. And still, no leads on who shot JuJu?"

"None."

We were both quiet for a while.

"Here. I'll wash your back."

Cage came closer to the tub and got on his knees. He took the rag out of my hand, and gently washed my back.

"Why couldn't I have met you like thirteen husbands ago?" I laughed at Cage.

"I don't know. I wish that it could've been under different circumstances, and not because I was doing my job; which, I still couldn't do, because I fell for you."

"Why?"

"Why what?"

"Why did you fall for me?"

"I don't know. Trust me, I didn't plan to. You reminded me of someone."

"Someone like who?"

"My wife. She died, years ago. She was pregnant. She was only six months. Her blood pressure was through the roof. We went to the hospital. She nor the baby came back out alive. I lost them both that night."

"I'm so sorry."

"It was a long time ago. But you somewhat reminded me of her. And the more we talked, the more I heard you laugh…"

Cage stopped talking. He finished washing my back and then he stood up.

"I'll go find you something to sleep in."

The rest of the night was pretty quiet between us, and it wasn't long before it was time for bed.

"I'll be on the couch, if you need me."

"I'd feel safer with you in the bed beside me."

Cage didn't comment.

He just crawled into the bed, without saying a word.

We faced each other, for a long time in silence.

I never knew that he'd been married.

Then again, there were a lot of things that he hadn't mentioned to me, before he revealed who he really was.

"She's kicking. Do you want to feel her?"

I could see Cage's teeth through the darkness. I felt for his hand, and then I placed it on my stomach.

"Do you feel it?"

"Yeah. I do."

He followed the kicks of his daughter, as I just laid there and allowed him to enjoy the moment.

After all, I wouldn't be around much longer for him to enjoy many more.

~***~

"Get down! Get down!"

Cage screamed, and slowly, I got down onto the floor. Cage left out of the bedroom. We'd heard the sound of shattered glass, and then a loud thud.

I sat on the floor, holding my belly. Soon, Cage appeared in the doorway of the room.

He was holding a brick.

"Well, someone knows that you are here.

He turned the brick to face me.

"I know you're in there."

Was written on a piece of paper, taped to the brick.

"They threw it through the living room window. It's cold. I need to get started patching it up. You stay in here," he said, sitting the brick down, and helping me onto the bed. "Don't come out until I say that it's okay," Cage closed the bedroom door.

I should've known that I'd been followed there. He, whoever he was, or maybe it was a she, always seemed to be watching and two steps ahead of me.

An hour or so later, Cage came back into the bedroom.

"Okay. I did what I could to it. I had a few things in the garage that I could work with. You can come out now if you want."

I didn't say anything.

Cage looked at me and saw that I was writing something.

"What's that?"

"I'm trying to make a list of who would be doing this, but I really don't know. I never had many friends, on purpose. I never stole a man from anyone, at least not that I know of, so I don't know who this could be. And I don't want you or anyone else to get hurt because of me."

I was frustrated.

At this point, I wanted to just turn my phone on and just tell whoever was giving me a hard time to just come and get me.

Shit! Just get it over with already.

"I can take care of myself."

He smiled at me.

I couldn't help, but to grin back.

"Thank you."

"For what?"

"I guess trying to save me. Trying to hide me. Trying to get Mama Kay's ashes for me. I never thanked you. So, thank you."

He didn't say anything for a while. "I want you to know something, Ivy." He said finally. "I believe you."

Maybe I was just overly emotional, or maybe my hormones got the best of me, but at his words, I scooted closer to him, and without hesitating, I kissed him.

Unlike the last time, without a second thought, Cage kissed me back. And for the next hour, the things that he did to me, and the way that he'd made me feel, couldn't quite be put into words. He satisfied me in a different way; not like the time before. He satisfied from a place of appreciation and purpose. He satisfied me from his soul. He gave me his body, gifted me pleasurable strokes and forgiving kisses. And I received them, all of them, and showed him my gratitude, as I came over and over again.

When we were finished, we just laid there, in each other's arms, unable to speak, unable to move. Unable to admit that the feeling, at that moment, was something that neither of us wanted to lose.

Even though we both knew that we had to.

~***~

It had been a week, since I'd been outside.

And it was snowing.

Every day, Cage came home saying that Nino was guarding the house like a watch dog, and every day, he told me to just leave the ashes behind.

And every day, I told him no.

I hadn't been on my phone, or anything, and I felt as though I was completely shut out from the outside world.

But I had to admit it, there with Cage, I felt safer than I'd felt in months. Maybe it was knowing that he was a cop, detective, or whatever he was, that gave me a sense of reassurance that no matter what happened, he would come out on top in the end.

I watched Cage pull into the driveway.

He got out of the car empty-handed again, but he walked fast as though he was in a hurry.

"Tell me where you plan to go. I'll get you the ashes. Just get your things, and let's go."

Cage moved hastily.

"What's wrong?"

"I met with Nino today. He asked me about you."

"Why?"

"He said that he got a random envelope the other day. Inside of it, were pictures of us, you and I, talking inside of the funeral home."

"What?"

"I saw them. Three photos. From that day. Someone must've taken them, or gotten them off of the camera. I can't be sure."

And my stalker strikes again!

"I told him that Sheree and I followed you there, which was the truth. And then I told him that I pretended to be the concerned ex-neighbor. I told him that we briefly talked about your mother, and what I'd heard about her death, and that was it. Honestly, I don't think he bought my story. I'm willing to bet that he will come snooping around."

I rolled my eyes. I wasn't scared of Nino, but I didn't want to be bothered with him either. Not now that I knew his true motives, and not now knowing that Cage truly believed that he could hurt me.

"Besides, it's time for me to go back home. The job has been up now for weeks, the department was paying the rent on this house. The job is over. The case is closed. So, it's time for me to go back home."

"Where is home?"

"My house, the one that I own, is about twenty minutes from here."

"And you've been pretending to live here? All of this time?"

"Being undercover is hard work. It isn't easy, not one bit," he commented.

He picked up the spare gun from the coffee table, just as there was a knock at the door.

We both looked at it.

Cage reached the gun to me, and after making sure that the safety was on, I placed it in the back of my jeans, near my right pocket.

"Who is it?"

"It's me! Open up." I could hear Sheree.

Cage motioned for me to go into the back room.

I just stood there.

"What are you doing? Open the door."

Cage looked at me and I looked back at him. I didn't want to hide from her. I'd spent the last week in his presence, and I didn't care if she knew that I was there. Besides, I was on my way out anyway. I was going to take Cage's advice and leave, and just send for Mama Kay's urn, when I could.

After Cage noticed that I wasn't going to move, he shook his head, and slowly opened the door.

"What's up?"

"What's up? Someone has been acting all strange lately," and she pushed past him and walked in. She froze once she saw me.

"What is she doing here?"

Cage glanced at me to see if I was going to answer. When I didn't, he answered her question.

"She just stopped by, we were just leaving."

She looked at Cage confused.

"Cage, what's going on?"

Cage reached me my small wristlet purse.

"Nino is still obsessing over the case."

Sheree opened her mouth.

"She knows."

She clamped her mouth shut.

"He can't accept the fact that the case is over. He basically held her hostage. She ran and came here. Now, she's about to leave."

"And go where?"

"Wherever. I'm just trying to get her out of here," Cage said.

Sheree still looked puzzled, but her next words surprised me.

"I can't let you do that."

"What?" Cage asked her.

Hastily, she drew her gun on him, and repeated herself. "I can't let you do that," and without hesitating, she shot him.

"Ahh!" I screamed as Cage hit the ground and then she pointed at me.

Here we go again.

"Come on. You're coming with me."

She held the gun towards me, and instinctively, I thought about JuJu and Mama Kay. I stepped over Cage as she opened the door.

"Come on."

"Where are you taking me?"

She told me to walk down the steps, and then she led me next door to my old house.

She kept me close to her as she opened the front door.

"Have a seat. Get comfortable. You're gonna be here for a while."

She waited for me to walk towards the couch and take a seat. It wasn't until I sat down that I remembered that I had the gun tucked away in my pants behind me.

"Why am I here?"

She chuckled. "You'll see." She took out her phone. "Hello. I have her."

Ah hell, she was helping Nino!

Once she was off of the phone, she sat on the couch across from me. When I was sure that she couldn't see the movement of my hand, I took the gun out of my jeans, and placed it in between the couch and my right thigh. I fiddled with the safety. Nino had never gotten around to teach me how to shoot, but Mama Kay had explained the basics.

"So, how many months along are you?"

"Enough. What is this about? Why are you keeping me here for him?"

"You'll see."

All was quiet for a while, and then she started to talk again.

"So, tell me something, did you really kill your husbands? That's what everyone wants to know. Were you setting it all up? Paying someone to take care of them? Making them look like accidents?"

I didn't answer her.

"Was it about money? Or did you just get bored?"

As she talked, I thought about Cage.

He was over there, bleeding to death, while she wanted to play a game of 21 questions.

"If I had been on this case from the beginning, you would've been in jail a long time ago."

I stared at her.

"I would've solved this. Cage wasn't the right man for the job. And neither was JuJu. She was so close to you, all of that time, and never found out anything that she could use. She didn't know what she was doing. She was just in the way."

Finally, something that caught my interest.

"You shot her...didn't you?"

"Yep. Like I said, she was in the way."

My blood boiled with fury.

"In the way?"

"Of the case. Of my money. Getting her out of the way, put me where I should've been in the first place."

Her phone vibrated, and I made sure that my hand stayed on the gun.

She listened to the voice on the other end.

"Well, it was nice talking to you, but my job is done."

She stood up, just as the front door opened.

I thought about pulling out the gun and shooting her, and then making a run for it, but I froze as he stepped inside.

What?

How?

Huh?

He walked in, as she headed out with a smile.

No.

This can't be.

I was so confused.

He stood there and allowed me to take it all in, but it just didn't make sense.

Right there. In the flesh. Stood my *supposed* to be dead husband...number...

****

Chapter EIGHT

"Hello, what is it...Ivy, now? I liked when you were going by Deena so much better. Surprised to see me, I can tell."

I'd stopped breathing for all of two minutes.

There he was, my ex-husband #9...

Dave.

Dave was the millionaire husband; the one who married me to cover-up his need for sexual relations with men. The husband that had tried to choke me to death. The husband who had committed suicide.

"What's wrong? Cat got your tongue?"

Dave walked closer to me.

"You're dead...you were dead. I saw you. I buried you."

"Or did you? A week with you away on that boat was plenty of time to make sure that when you got back, that you saw what I wanted to see. When you have enough money, anything is possible; especially faking your death. People do it all the time. They even have experts that help you out and shit. Bet you didn't know that, did you?"

Dave looked exactly the same.

He didn't look as though he'd aged even a day, even though it had been years. He was still handsome, overdressed, and he still walked like he was the finest man in the room, which usually, he was.

For a white guy, he'd had a certain type of swag that I'd liked. The kind that you couldn't resist.

Flabbergasted, I didn't know what to say, as he stood right in front of me.

"I've waited a long time for this. For this moment. To see the look on your face that you have right now."

"So, the suicide note, the pills, were all lies?"

"After that bitch of a mother of yours hit me over the head, God rest her soul…nah, I take that back. I never liked her anyway. Hours later, I received those little messages that you had sent to me. The pictures and videos, no need to go over what there were, or who they were with, you know that already, but you also know that they would've ruined me."

I didn't know what the hell he was talking about.

"I don't know who you had following me, or who you'd had to take them, but when I read those messages, saying that they would leak them, if I didn't knock myself off, I was stuck between a rock and a hard place. Imagine having the choice whether to kill yourself, or have your entire life, and everything that you've worked for, stripped away from you in an instant. That's a hell of a choice, don't you think? And it was the only choice that you gave to me. I could tell that it wasn't you sending the messages, but I knew that you were behind them, especially when you mentioned the choking."

That must've been Mama Kay, unless she'd told someone else what to say.

"The messages even told me which one of my prescriptions to use to do it. They told me how many pills to take to get the job done. Now, that is some fucked up shit!"

I swear, Mama Kay didn't used to miss a thing!

Of course, I hadn't taken pictures or videos, and I had no idea what he was doing behind my back, until I went through his phone, but obviously, Mama Kay had.

"I mean, I knew that you were pissed about the video and the choking thing, but I didn't know that you'd had those type of balls on you. And I didn't know that you had that type of dirt on me, or your plans to use it. Even with the messages staring me in my face, I still doubted you. Until you or whoever you had messaging me, sent me a list of media contacts, big media contacts, that you already had on speed dial. You, or whoever, already had the e-mail typed and ready to send out them, with the pictures and videos already attached. The press would've gone crazy! My father would've been shamed. Not only would he have disowned me, but the business would've suffered, all because of me. He, nor anyone else in my family, would've ever forgiven me. I wasn't sure if I wanted to live with that type of guilt. And then, the last message confirmed again, the number of pills that I needed to take to make my heart stop beating, and it said for me to write a suicide note; so, that I could tell the story, my truth, in my own way. And if I didn't, if I wasn't dead when you got back, life as I knew it, would be over."

The tone in Dave's voice had changed.

He was still angry. And maybe a tad bit hurt.

Mama Kay had never told me so many details, so a lot of what I was hearing, was new.

She'd always shielded me from what she did and how she did it, just in case something ever went wrong. Well, it did. Something went wrong…and he was standing right in front of me.

"I had to make a hard decision. But I made the only choice that I felt like I had. Let's face it, my father was a pain in my ass. So much so, that I'd started embezzling money from the company, for years, as a backup plan. I had plenty of money, with or without being in his will, and enough money to disappear forever, without having to live in his shadow; without being judged. And let's face it, embezzlement isn't all that easy to swing, so, I assumed that one day it would catch up with me, and considering that, and considering everything, and since you left me no choice, I did what I had to do. I faked my death. All of it, every last bit of it, was staged. The reporters that had gotten inside of the house, had been paid. The photos had been manipulated. Making my parents, verify my body from behind a glass window, so that they couldn't see my small breaths, was staged. The mortician, and his suggestion of having me a closed casket service due to rapid decaying, was planned. It wasn't me in that box. My funeral was all a show. I spent a whole lot of money, to fool a whole lot of people…all because of you."

Wow!

That was my first thought. He'd pulled it off. He'd fooled me and everyone else. And even with him standing in front of me, half of my mind was still in disbelief.

My second thought made me uncomfortable. I already knew that only one of us would be leaving this room alive.

"You see, I fell off of the map, able to live free from judgement, rich, and comfortable, but I couldn't forget about you. Oh no. My death made you a very rich woman. And while I was on the beaches of Peru, I thought about how much control I'd allowed you to have over the situation. I'd allowed you to make a decision for me. What kind of man would I be to tuck in my tail like that and just roll over to some bitch? Some bitch that was now living it large, with a few millions of my money?"

He slapped me upside of the head, literally, and it caught me off guard.

"Keep your hands off of me!"

"Or what?"

I didn't answer him, so he kept right on talking.

"I left you alone for a long while, but I was just waiting on the right time. I was waiting for my moment. I hired a few people to do a lot digging for me. And the deeper and deeper they went, the more and more they found. I discovered all of the husbands before me. I found out that they were all dead, and I told myself: she's done this before. She's going to do it again. And I was right. You did. You did it, again, and again, and again. Come on now, you needed to be stopped. And that's my purpose in life…to stop you."

"You don't know what you're talking about."

"Oh. But I do. I found out everything that I could on you. Even gave you the truth about your dear old mother, as a little present. How about a thank you? She'd lied about your father, and apparently, you had a sister who just dropped off of the map in the 80's. I wonder what happened to little ole' Daisy."

At first, I was confused, but then I chuckled.

Even he didn't catch that Mama Kay *was* Daisy. He'd actually mistaken her for our mother and just assumed that she'd lied about who my father was and about me having a sister. It just showed how much she truly did look like our real mother.

"She'd lied about who your father was, because he was dead too. Some ladder accident. A whole lot of accidents happen in your family, doesn't it?"

Dave started to pace back and forth.

"I watched you. Kept tabs on you. I knew every time that you got married. Every time that you moved to a different state and when you changed your name. This time, this last time, I found out about the investigation, and thought that it was time to make my move. I had to get in on the action. I couldn't just let the police have all of the fun. I was too invested. Sheree. She's one of my connections. She was the one that told me that they were going to start building a case on you. Showtime."

Dave chuckled, crazily, I focused on holding my pee, but I kept my eyes on him, and my hand on the piece of steel.

"I flew my handsome, supposed to be dead, self, all the way here, to join in on the fun. Just to start some trouble."

Now, everything made sense.

"You knew that Nino, Cage, JuJu, were all working to bring me down?"

"Yep. And for a while I was enjoying the show, but it needed a little entertainment. The excitement was missing. I was missing."

"The e-mails? The incidents with Nino? Sneaking around our house? All of the random things? Following me? That was all you?"

"Guilty." Dave raised his hand.

"And that night…in my bedroom…"

"That dick felt good, didn't it?"

I became as hot as hen's piss with his words.

"I've always liked kitty cat, the most. It was always my first choice. You just couldn't seem to get with the program."

There it was. There was the truth.

Every last, twisted, psycho, surprising bit of it!

"I enjoyed watching the panic. I enjoyed watching you live in wonder and in fear. I convinced Sheree to shoot JuJu, just so that I could see you in more pain. Just so I could take someone away from you. I'll admit, she wanted to do it anyway. And Nino, he was just collateral damage. He is a tough son-of-a bitch, though. He just wouldn't die! Disappointing."

Dave started coming towards me again.

"But with all things, they must come to an end. I've obsessed over you for far too long. There's an island and a jack and coke, calling my name. I just have to finish up one little thing first," Dave moved so quickly, that I hadn't had time to think.

He had his hands around my neck again, causing me to relive the memories from the first time around, all over again.

"I've waited years to do this. To finish what I'd started that night. There's no one here to save you now, is there?"

Dave squeezed so hard, that my hands seemed to go numb. After a while, I patted for the gun, but from the pressure of his body, and from the tightness around my throat, I couldn't seem to grip that I needed.

"All you had to do was be a good wife. A silent and understanding wife. Was that too much to ask? I gave you everything you wanted. Everything you needed. All you had to do was keep your mouth shut!"

Dave squeezed as he talked, and I continued to push and claw at him with my left hand.

I started to see the light, or maybe it was a vision, but I was giving up, just like I had before. I had a quick vision of the baby. She had to be around four or five years old.

She was running, and I was chasing behind her on a hot summer's day. Maybe that's what we would do in Heaven, I concluded. Maybe Mama Kay was there and waiting for me.

"If it's any consolation, you were my favorite wife. It's funny. I loved and hated you the most! Oh well, Goodbye Malaysia Christina. Goodbye Deanna Marie. And Goodbye Ivy Raye! Goodbye and good rid---"

Just then, the front door kicked open.

Dave turned towards it and once his hands loosened up, immediately I gasped for air.

I heard talking, but I couldn't understand what was being said. I was too busy breathing and reaching beside of my leg, for the gun and once my finger found the trigger…

BANG!

Dave was still leaning over me, and I pulled the trigger again.

I could hear voices, yelling, but I was staring into Dave's eyes. I wanted to make sure that his death, was done right this time, so I squeezed the trigger again.

Police swarmed all around us, and though I was somewhat in a trance, I felt my lips curl up into a small smile, as I watched Dave bleed out all over me.

He looked at me, with a crooked smile.

"Game over," he mumbled.

"I win," I said back to him, as he clutched his chest and slid down to the floor, silently.

I was still out of it, as I started to feel the tugging.

I felt myself being pulled towards the front door, but for a while, I kept my eyes on Dave. The cold air slammed against my sweating body, and finally, I was able to take in what was going on around me.

Immediately, I spotted Cage. He lifted up off of the stretcher at the sight of me.

I saw Sheree in the back of a police car. She glared at me and I waved my middle finger at her.

Cops were all over me. The entire neighborhood was either on their porches, or piled up in the middle of the street. I watched Nino come out of the house and head towards me.

A few more cops and medics ran inside.

Nino searched for me, and when he found my eyes, he headed in my direction.

"Sheree told us that he's one of your ex-husbands. One that you thought was dead."

I didn't reply to him.

He sounded different.

As though he was relieved. As though he was done pretending.

The cops started to put my hands behind my back, but Nino shook his head.

"I guess by now, you know that, I'm not who you thought I was."

"No one is ever who they appear to be."

I thought about something.

"Were we ever really married? Legally?"

"Depends on how you look at it. Nino isn't even my real name," he confessed.

I didn't say anything to him.

"Cage told us that Sheree shot him, and then took you. She was going to let him kill you, and from the looks of your neck, he almost did."

The medics started to touch all over me. They checked my neck and wanted to check out my stomach.

"Sir, he's dead," a cop said, approaching the man that I called Nino.

Another cop tried to put me in handcuffs again, but he shook his head.

"She's going to the hospital…not to jail. What she did in there, was self-defense. Can't deny the truth when it's something that you see for yourself," Nino confirmed.

I still couldn't bring myself to speak again.

I was still in complete shock at what had taken place.

Dave being alive, all this time, was still hard for me to take in; even with his blood all over me.

They started to lead me to the ambulance and then they got me comfortable on the stretcher.

Nino just stood there, looking at me. He knew that this was goodbye, but I could tell that a part of him, didn't want to say it.

And he didn't.

Finally, he turned away from me.

"Ay."

He turned around, at the sound of my voice.

"I guess now I can finally say what you have always wanted to hear me say."

Nino didn't say anything.

"Ask me again."

He looked perplexed.

"Ask me the question, again."

I could tell that he was wondering if I was serious.

I was.

"Ivy, did you kill your husbands?"

I watched the men, drag the big black bag into the house that they were going to put Dave's body in. Once they disappeared, I looked back at Nino, and answered his question.

"No. I only killed one of them. But I wish that I'd killed two," I glared at him, hoping that he understood, my animosity towards him.

Nino looked at me, smirked, took off his ring, and stepped on it with his shoe.

"Well, lucky for you, from this moment on, husband #13, is officially dead…too," he walked away from me, confirming that the past two years, that he'd spent with me, was just a job and that to him, it hadn't…I hadn't…meant a thing.

~***~

8 Amazing Months Later...

"I hate sand," he said and I turned around.

I couldn't believe my eyes.

It was Cage.

It had been months since I'd left him, and everything else back in Virginia behind.

I was trying to move on with my life. I was trying to forget the past, and everything else that had come along with it.

Cage sat down beside of me. The baby cooed.

"How did you find me?"

For a moment, he couldn't take his eyes off of the baby.

"It took a while. I asked for you as soon as I opened up my eyes, after surgery. At the hospital, that day. You were gone. I'd hoped that you would've at least said goodbye," he said.

The waves crashed against the beach, and the cool breeze tickled the hairs in my nose.

"I knew that you would change your name. I knew that you wouldn't want to be found. But I looked for you anyway. I tried to trace your last steps. I'd even gone by your house to see if you had gone to get the urn, you had. I knew right then, that you were gone. I knew that you had disappeared. But with a little determination, I kept looking."

His chocolate skin glistened in the sunlight. His hair was loose, and his curls were swaying all over the place, and the scent coming from his skin, instinctively, made my mouth start to water.

"I came across a picture. A photo. I brought it with me." He took the photo out of his pocket.

It was the family photo of me, Mama Kay, and our parents. I'd always regretted leaving it behind.

"I remembered your sister comment. It took me a while to put it all together, but I did. *She* was your sister. Mama Kay. The whole time, she wasn't your mother, she was your sister."

For some strange reason, I smiled at him.

I wasn't sure why, but I did. I rocked the baby back and forth. I could tell that he was dying to hold her, but he kept talking instead.

"After I put that together, I did some more digging. And then some more digging. And then one day, it just hit me. You loved your Mama, sister, you know; you loved her so much. So much, that you wouldn't even get yourself to safety without her ashes. And after finding out that her, your sister's, real name was Daisy June, I was sure that would be your new name. But I was wrong. Instead, that's what you named the baby."

He touched his daughter's hand.

"When I saw a Daisy June Banks, born just five months ago, all the way in Hawaii, I knew that it was her. I knew that I'd found you. I sold everything. Quit my job. I didn't tell anyone, anything, other than a few family members, so that they wouldn't be worried about me. I told them that I was going away for a while, and that I would call them, from time to time. And then I came here, and I found you. And I'm not leaving here without you, without her. And if you want to stay here, fine, then I'm staying here too."

I shook my head.

"Cage."

"I'm not leaving you Ivy...or should I call you, what is it now, Lani? I'm not leaving you. Ever. I won't, I can't live without her."

He reached for her, and to my surprise, she came to him. I looked at him in disbelief.

After everything, through all of the trouble, death and sin. In some weird way, he was still offering to be with me, until the end.

"Where have you been all my life?" I laughed.

"I was right next door. And now I'm right here. All that matters, to me, is right here."

I stared at him in amazement.

I knew that he'd meant every word that he'd said.

"Okay, you can stay. But under one condition. No matter what happens, no matter where life takes us, Cage, I don't ever, ever, EVER want to get married again," I said.

"Good." He chuckled. "That means that I won't end up dead."

****

THE END

Check out these books next:

The Hidden Wife

The Wrong Husband

The Golden Lie

The Janes

Your Pastor My Husband

AND MANY MORE!

CPSIA information can be obtained
at www.ICGtesting.com
Printed in the USA
BVHW04s0050130618
518930BV00001B/12/P

9 781981 244843